D1686360

Irish Tearoom Mysteries

DIGGING UP DANGER

Elizabeth Penney

Annie's®
AnniesFiction.com

Books in the Irish Tearoom Mysteries series

A Deadly Brew
Steeped in Lies
Yule Pay Dearly
Claddagh in Secrecy
Druid on Arrival
Cottage in the Act
Final Resting Lace
Tempers in a Teapot
Infused With Murder
Digging Up Danger
A Knife to Remember
Wed and Gone

... and more to come!

Digging Up Danger
Copyright © 2025 Annie's.

All rights reserved. No part of this publication may be reproduced, stored in a retrieval system, or transmitted in any form or by any means—electronic, mechanical, photocopying, recording or otherwise—without the prior written permission of the publisher. The only exception is brief quotations in printed reviews. For information address Annie's, 306 East Parr Road, Berne, Indiana 46711-1138.

The characters and events in this book are fictional, and any resemblance to actual persons or events is coincidental.

Library of Congress-in-Publication Data
Digging Up Danger / by Elizabeth Penney
p. cm.
ISBN: 979-8-89253-316-4
I. Title
2023940671

AnniesFiction.com
Irish Tearoom Mysteries™
Series Creator: Shari Lohner
Series Editor: Elizabeth Morrissey
Cover Illustrator: Gregory Copeland

10 11 12 13 14 | Printed in China | 9 8 7 6 5 4 3 2 1

1

Penny Cavanagh watched with bated breath as her cousin Nora Murphy forced the last bag into her silver Peugeot's rear cargo area then stood back, hands on hips.

"I think that's everything," Nora announced. She closed the hatch with an extra push to help it shut all the way.

Penny laughed, glad all of their luggage fit in the compact car. "I certainly hope so."

The cousins were taking a trip to Ireland's northwestern coast to join an Iron Age archaeological dig at the invitation of one of Nora's college friends. Although the cousins didn't have any background in archaeology, Nora was a talented painter who would be acting as the dig's sketch artist while Penny would be the group's cook, both of them temporarily replacing regular members taking time off.

Since moving from San Diego back to her native Blarney Green, a quaint County Cork village on the island's southern end, Penny had spent most of her time working in her family's tearoom, The Merry Teapot, and reacclimating to life in Ireland after being away since her childhood. Not to mention solving a few murders. With any luck, a weeklong working vacation would give her a break from that in particular.

Nora leaned halfway into the back seat to get her wheaten terrier, Corky, settled for the trip. Penny heard the sound of an engine coming up the drive of the stone tower house—some might call it a miniature castle—she shared with Nora. Their driveway was a quarter mile long, edged by woods, so she couldn't see the vehicle until it reached the house.

A vintage Morris Minor Traveller drove into view, its powder-blue paint color a few shades lighter than the August sky. The women's grandmother, Nan Murphy, was at the wheel, and she waved as she pulled to a stop. Penny and Nora exchanged worried glances. Had a last-minute problem popped up that would force them to cancel their trip?

"Good morning, Nan," Nora called. "Is everything all right?"

"It's grand," Nan said as she climbed out of the Traveller. Petite and spry, Nan sported a head of red hair similar to Nora's, though Nan depended on dye to achieve the color. She believed the tourists at the tearoom expected to see red hair in Ireland. She opened the rear door and extracted a picnic basket. "I wanted to bring you a few treats for the ride."

"How thoughtful," Penny said, hurrying forward to take the basket.

Their journey to Anoach Island, north of Galway and connected to the mainland by a causeway, would take much of the day. They could use extra goodies to snack on, especially if they'd been made by Nan or The Merry Teapot's pastry chef, Cedric O'Reilly. Penny made room in the back seat for the basket. Corky sniffed curiously for a moment before resettling himself in his spot.

"Good boy, Corky," Penny murmured before she withdrew from the car.

Gravel crunching under tires announced another car coming up the driveway.

"Who is that now?" Nora asked.

"It's Finn," Penny announced, her heart lifting as she spotted the Toyota SUV belonging to Finn Campbell, the local detective inspector and her steady boyfriend. Tall and athletic with cropped strawberry-blond hair, he was as handsome as he was dedicated to his job protecting the citizens of Blarney Green.

Finn rolled to a stop, then hopped out. "Bon voyage party?" he asked, green eyes twinkling.

After exchanging greetings with everyone, he opened his back door and pulled out a small shopping bag. He walked toward Penny while Nan and Nora launched into conversation about the tearoom.

"I brought you a small gift," Finn said. "Sorry I didn't have time to wrap it."

Penny couldn't hold back a grin. "You didn't have to do that."

He shrugged as he handed her the bag. "I know. I wanted to."

Penny's grin widened when she saw what it contained. "How thoughtful," she said, pulling out a pair of compact binoculars. She put them up to her eyes to try them out.

"You can use them for bird-watching," Finn suggested. "Or to spot whales and dolphins."

Still holding the glasses, Penny threw her arms around his neck. "Thank you," she said, then added in a whisper, "I'm going to miss you."

"And I you," he whispered back. "But it'll pass quick as a flash. I hope you have a wonderful time. Besides, I'll see you soon." The plan was for Finn to come to Anoach Island at the end of the week, spend a couple of days relaxing there, and then drive Penny home. Nora was going to stay on for another week.

Finn approached Nora's car to pet Corky, who had stuck his head out of the open window. "You ready for an adventure, buddy?"

"He's going to have the time of his life," Penny said. "We'll be working outside, so he'll get plenty of fresh air and exercise."

"Have fun, Corky," Finn said with a final pat. He returned his attention to Penny. "I'd best be off. I'm headed to the station to wrap things up before my training course starts in Galway."

Penny was glad Finn's advanced detective training would be at the same time as her trip and that its location on the west coast made it convenient for him to join her afterward. "I hope it goes well."

"Thank you. I'm looking forward to it." After giving Penny a prolonged hug and giving well wishes to Nora and Nan, Finn climbed back into the SUV and drove away.

"Is anyone else coming?" Nan asked, putting a hand behind her ear. "No, I guess not. I'd better be away as well. Have a wonderful time, my *colleens*." She punctuated the Irish word for *girls* or *young women* with a kiss on each of their cheeks. "And keep in touch with your old grandmother."

Penny and Nora laughed. "You're not old, Nan," Penny said. "We'll text you when we get there, okay?"

"Our best to everyone at the tearoom," Nora said.

"And the cats," Penny added. She'd miss Nan's cats, Earl and Grey, but was glad to have Corky along for company.

Nora and Penny stood together, waving while the Traveller ambled down the drive. As the sound of the vehicle died in the distance, Nora faced Penny. "One more quick check and we'll go."

"I'm going to make sure the kettle is off," Penny said, trotting toward the kitchen door.

Nora glanced up from the packing list she was consulting, a wry grin quirking her lips. "Nothing wrong with that, even though we've both checked it twice."

A short while later, they were on their way with Nora at the wheel, Penny in the passenger seat, and Corky curled up in a ball on the back seat. Penny opened her window and enjoyed the breeze on her face. Adventure and the open road lay ahead.

They merged onto the highway in Cork City, heading due north through the heart of the Emerald Isle. The driving was more relaxed on the busy road, with no stray sheep or pedestrians to worry about.

"How did you meet Oliver Turnbull?" Penny asked, sipping from her travel mug of tea. "I wouldn't think an archaeology major and an art school student would have much occasion to cross paths."

Nora sipped from her own thermos. "We lived in the same building. One night his flatmates had a party and he invited me. After that, we became quite good friends."

Penny wondered if there had been a spark between the pair. Over the years, Nora had dated plenty but had never found anyone she wanted to settle down with.

"I know what you're thinking," Nora said. "I call that your matchmaking face."

"Really?" Penny carefully rearranged her features. "I wasn't aware I had such a thing." Before moving to Ireland, Penny had operated a matchmaking service in San Diego. A high-profile match gone terribly wrong had been one reason she'd sought a change of scenery in her native Ireland. She had intended to visit temporarily while she decided what to do, but she had fallen in love with her new community and had made her stay permanent.

"Oliver and I were friends. He was like a brother to me, actually. A brother who wasn't as annoying as my own." Nora wrinkled her nose at the mention of her six brothers who, though they were all adults between the ages of twenty-six and thirty-seven, had been a boisterous bunch as youngsters and hadn't done much to shake the reputation they'd built. "I've always been fascinated by archaeology, so we spent a lot of time talking about what he was learning."

"I didn't realize they still used artists at digs," Penny said. "I assumed that with advances in digital photography, drawings would be redundant."

"It's a tradition," Nora said. "Plus, illustrations capture details that aren't so obvious in photos. Some objects don't photograph well.

I'm excited that I finally get to do it, even for a little bit while their artist is on medical leave. It's a dream come true."

"I'm excited that you asked me along. I've always been fascinated by archaeology too. I wish I'd been there when they opened King Tut's tomb to see all those precious gems and gold."

"And don't forget the everyday objects," Nora said. "We can learn a lot about life in the past through those. Even about the food they ate."

"Always of interest to me," Penny agreed. "Don't they analyze mummies to see what their diets were?"

Nora nodded. "Hair, bones, and teeth hold a lot of information. That's why bog bodies are so valuable."

"Bog bodies?" The term sounded somewhat familiar to Penny. "What are those?"

"Exactly what they sound like—people buried in peat bogs. The peat releases acid as it decomposes, which preserves them amazingly well. Haven't you heard of the famous Lady of the Bog?"

"Hold on." Penny put her cup in the holder and picked up her phone. A couple of minutes later, she found a site that explained the Lady, who was estimated to be from around 200 BCE. Her heart gave a leap. "She was found on Anoach Island. That's where we're going."

"They discovered her in the early 1900s. And I understand that they've made quite a cottage industry out of her. Everything on the island is all about the Lady of the Bog. There's even a museum."

"Wow. She's an attraction?" While traveling the United States, Penny had seen some unusual and even humorous roadside attractions, but a preserved body extracted from a peat bog topped them all.

"I guess you could call her that. She's rare and remarkable. People travel from all over to see her."

Penny set her phone aside and picked up her tea. "So, back to Oliver. You're sure he's only a friend?"

Nora snorted. "Absolutely. Though he is gorgeous. Girls were always pursuing him." She fiddled with the airflow knobs. "Especially Caroline, who finally caught him."

Penny recognized the subtle curl of Nora's lip. "You don't like Caroline."

Nora didn't answer directly. "They got married after college. Caroline is also an archaeologist. However, they recently split up."

"Who left whom?" Penny asked, curious.

"Caroline left Oliver. Apparently she thought he wasn't ambitious enough. She had visions of the pair of them traveling the world. Oliver is content to focus on his region of interest—Great Britain and Ireland."

"Sounds like her loss." Penny already felt loyal to Nora's friend, trusting her cousin's character judgment.

"I'll say. That's another reason I'm going. Oliver was pretty devastated by the whole thing, and he needs a friend right now."

"You'll straighten him out." Penny was confident that Nora's brand of forthright common sense and optimism would do Oliver a world of good.

In the back seat, Corky whined. Nora glanced in the rearview mirror. "Ready for a break, boy? We'll stop in a few minutes to stretch your legs."

Penny pulled up a map to view their journey. They were headed to Limerick and then to Galway, where the route would begin to take them northwest. Anoach Island was off the westernmost "bump" on the Irish coastline.

"Lunch in Limerick?" Penny suggested.

"Sounds good. I know a great tearoom there." Nora's expression was mischievous. "It's always good to check out the competition."

The tearoom was old-fashioned and charming, despite being in the middle of the city, and there were outside tables so Corky could stay with them, his leash secured to a chair. A few crumbs of Penny's potato cakes and Nora's ploughman's lunch landed on the sidewalk near his nose, disappearing quickly.

Their server was interested to learn that they were from Blarney Green and had heard of The Merry Teapot, which pleased Penny and Nora. They took a couple photos in front of the tearoom and sent them to Nan.

Missing me already, are you? Nan texted back quickly.

Of course! was the cousins' enthusiastic reply.

After a peek at King John's Castle with its squat, round towers, they resumed their journey. North of Galway, the highway became a regular two-way road again. They passed through small towns built close to the road between stretches of green countryside. The road grew even narrower still as they approached the headlands close to the sea.

Every so often, Penny caught glimpses of the water as they passed through various port towns. At one point, they had a view of islands in the bay, cast like green jewels on a blue background. Farther on, mountains rose from the coastal plain, part of a national park featuring peat bogs, migratory birds, and salmon rivers, according to Nora. Signs of civilization became sparser, and Penny realized how remote the region was.

"I should have stopped for petrol," Nora said with a huff of annoyance. "I'm not sure what's available on the island. Keep your eyes open for a station, will you?"

Penny hoped they'd see one, since the last sizable settlement had been ten kilometers back the other way. "You aren't going to run out, I hope."

"No. But I'd like to fill up before we head to the island."

Anxiously watching the roadside, Penny spotted a modern store with canopies up ahead. "There's one. Dungsley Fuel and Convenience."

Nora pulled into a slot at the pumps. After filling the Peugeot's tank, they went inside for snacks to add to Nan's picnic basket, the contents of which they'd grazed on during the drive. Among the typical packaged snacks, the convenience store offered locally baked pastries, and Penny selected a couple of golden-brown sausage rolls that smelled tasty.

"Where are you headed?" asked the middle-aged man at the till. "Here for the park?"

"We're actually joining the dig on Anoach," Nora answered.

The man's bushy gray brows went up. "Searching for a new Lady, are you?" He jerked his thumb at fanciful posters featuring an Iron Age queen with cloak and spear. Once she took that in, Penny noticed a lot of other items with the picture, including key chains, mugs, magnets, and shirts.

"I don't think that's the priority," Nora said. "We're excavating a village. Besides, there's no evidence that the Lady was a warrior."

"Who says she wasn't?" the man said, his thick lower lip pouting. "No proof of that."

"Fair enough," Nora conceded. "In any case, she's a significant find."

"She is indeed. We're quite proud of her around here." He tipped his head. "Good luck with the dig."

They thanked him as they gathered their purchases and left. Outside the store, Penny said, "He was a little touchy about the Lady."

"I'll say." Nora laughed. "Let that be a warning to you."

Penny had been other places where a figure, human or animal, was considered iconic. In Anoach, it was the Lady of the Bog. Before they left, she'd buy some souvenirs for Finn and for her family in the United States. They would get a kick out of it.

Corky whined when he smelled the sausage rolls. "Hold tight," Nora told him. "We'll give you dinner when we get there." With a lick of his chops, he settled down again.

"Not much farther, right?" Penny asked.

"Only a few more miles." Nora sighed as she started the car. "I'm ready to stop driving myself."

"I'll bet." Despite her tiredness, Penny felt a fresh rush of energy as they crossed the causeway to the island. She took deep breaths of salty air. "I love the ocean."

"Me too," Nora said. "Hopefully I can do some painting while I'm here."

Once across the bridge, the lane became even narrower, often hemmed in with stone walls or hedges. Rocks and boulders dotted the uneven fields, the landscape far different from the sleek, prosperous farms near Blarney Green.

"The road to the caravan park where we're staying should be here somewhere," Nora muttered, glancing at a printed map she'd brought along in case her GPS didn't work in the remote location. She handed Penny the page. "Can you figure out where?"

"I'll try." Penny studied the map, taking a moment to orient herself. "We need to watch for Cillian's Bog Road. Hopefully there's a marker."

Nora slowed as the road became winding and hilly, driving carefully to avoid colliding with any vehicles coming around a bend.

Penny spotted a brown heap lying in the road a distance ahead. "What's that?" Her stomach rolled. Had an animal been hit?

Nora hit the brakes. As they rolled to a halt, the object came into focus. Nora gasped. "It's a man."

Penny's heart clenched with horror. Was he dead?

2

Penny opened the car door and jumped out, praying that the man was alive. Had he been struck by a car? Was he ill?

Nora raced with her to check on the man. "Call for help," Nora said as she bent to examine him. She put fingers to his neck. "He's warm and has a pulse," she reported, then raised her voice. "Can you hear me, sir?"

After returning to the car for her phone, Penny dialed the emergency number with shaking fingers, glad they had service in such a remote area. As the phone rang, she realized she had no idea where they were. Before she could ask Nora, the dispatcher picked up and asked the purpose for her call.

"This is Penny Cavanagh," she said. "We're on Anoach Island. Hold on, I don't know exactly—"

"About five miles from the causeway, on Lewis Hill Lane," Nora called.

Penny repeated that. "We came across a man lying in the road. We think he might have been hit by a car."

"You hit him with your car?" the dispatcher asked.

"No," Penny said, alarmed. "He had already been hit when we found him."

"We'll send an ambulance and the Garda," the dispatcher said. "Stay where you are."

"We will. Thank you." After disconnecting, Penny walked over to join Nora. "You won't believe . . ."

Penny's words trailed off when she noticed the expression of disbelief on her cousin's face.

"Penny, I know him."

"What?" Penny studied the man. He had rugged features and a large, graying mustache. He wore light trousers, a windbreaker, and hiking shoes. She'd never seen him before. "Is he from Blarney Green?"

"No," Nora said, shaking her head. "He's the leader of the dig. Kenneth McCarty. I haven't met him in person, but I recognize him from the website."

As if in response, Kenneth groaned, rolling his head back and forth.

"Don't move, Kenneth," Nora said. "You're hurt."

"The ambulance will be here soon," Penny chimed in.

Kenneth opened his eyes, which were a pale, watery blue. "What happened?"

"You must have been hit by a car," Penny said gently. "Unless you fell down." *Or had a heart attack*, she realized. "How's your chest?"

Kenneth breathed deeply a few times. "Everything hurts except my chest. I'm voting for being hit by a car." He closed his eyes again, seeming to lapse into unconsciousness.

Nora threw a worried glance up the lane. "I hope they get here soon." She rose to her feet and took out her phone. "I'm calling Oliver. He needs to hear about this."

She strode a short distance away, pacing back and forth while she waited for the call to connect. "Oliver, it's Nora. Yes, we're on the island. Kenneth has been hurt. We found him lying in the road."

Even from a distance, Penny heard Oliver's squawk of alarm.

"Yes, I'm serious. The ambulance is coming." Nora gave him their location and said, "Okay, see you soon." She marched back over to Penny. "He's on his way."

Maybe Oliver could shed some light on the situation—for example, why Kenneth was on the road on foot. Perhaps he'd been walking somewhere, such as the grocery store or to visit somebody. Or he could have been in a car with someone, they'd argued, and then the person had decided to run him over.

"It's really quiet out here," Nora said after a moment. "I can't believe we haven't seen another vehicle the whole time we've been here."

Penny agreed with Nora's assessment. Besides a bird chirping in a nearby apple tree, the lone sound was the wind, which was incessant and smelled of salt. She imagined that steady wind scouring the landscape, twisting the trees, blowing soil away to expose the island's bony back.

In the distance, something whined. "There's Oliver," Nora said.

A motorcycle soon appeared on the road, the noise growing as it raced toward them. He roared right up to them before swerving sharply and coming to a halt. The engine cut, and he pulled off his helmet and raised his goggles, revealing a thatch of brown hair, hazel eyes, and thin, expressive features.

Oliver hopped off the bike and hurried over. "Kenneth," he said, hunkering down. "Are you all right?"

"He's unconscious now, but he did speak to us a few minutes ago," Nora said. Gnawing at her lip, she scanned their surroundings. "Where on earth is that ambulance?"

When a siren sounded in the distance, Penny felt her shoulders relax. "There they are."

"It takes a bit," Oliver said. "They're headquartered off the island." He proceeded to check Kenneth's pulse. "Hang in there, old man. We'll get you fixed up."

"Do you know why he was out here?" Nora asked.

Oliver shook his head. "Not specifically. Kenneth liked to take long walks, though. He's covered most of this island, I'd say."

The ambulance and a Garda vehicle approached from the same direction Nora and Penny had been traveling. "Should I move my car?" Nora asked. Where she was stopped, there wasn't room for the ambulance to go around.

"I'd wait," Penny said, the dispatcher's accusatory words fresh in her mind. "They're probably going to examine it."

"Why?" Nora frowned, then understanding dawned. "We did not hit him."

Two gardaí, one male and one female, and two medics approached.

"What happened here?" the male garda asked. He was on the short side yet muscular, with a bit of a swagger. His name badge identified him as Sergeant Miles Chambley.

"We came across Kenneth lying in the road as we drove by," Nora said. "We were on our way to join the dig."

The medics went over to Kenneth and began examining him.

Sergeant Chambley's brows went up. "You know the man?"

"Allow me, Sergeant," the other garda said. Tall, thin, and tan, she had a sharp gaze and lean, attractive features. "I'm Detective Inspector Arlene Babcock. You are?"

The medics went to get a gurney, preparing to take Kenneth to the hospital.

"Nora Murphy and Penny Cavanagh," Nora said, gesturing. "We're from Blarney Green, County Cork."

"We hired Nora as a sketch artist," Oliver put in. "Penny is working for us too."

The medics were ready to transport Kenneth, so the inspector excused herself to talk to them. Once Kenneth was loaded in the ambulance, the two gardaí began to examine Nora's car. Corky, startled, began to bark.

"Thank goodness I don't have any dents," Nora said in a low voice.

Oliver frowned. "Want me to set them straight?"

Nora put a hand on his arm. "Please don't. They're doing their job." She faced the car and called, "It's okay, Corky. We'll let you out soon." The dog quieted.

The ambulance began to roll away, the siren blaring. Penny hoped that Kenneth would make a full recovery. She wondered if he'd seen the vehicle that hit him. Otherwise, it might be impossible to find the driver responsible.

The two gardaí came back. "Nice dog," Chambley said. "My mam has a wheaten terrier too."

Nora smiled in acknowledgment. "Corky is a good boy."

"We don't see any signs of damage on your vehicle, so you are free to go," Detective Inspector Babcock said. "First, I'm going to need your contact information."

"Gladly," Penny said, then recited her and Nora's phone numbers. "We hope you find out who hit Kenneth. It's horrible that they drove away like that and left him in the road." She thought of something. "By the way, do you know Detective Inspector Finn Campbell from Blarney Green?" She didn't generally share personal information, but thought it might give her and Nora a little credibility.

"We've met," Babcock said.

"He's my boyfriend," Penny told her. "I'll be sure to tell him that we ran into you." *Unfortunate choice of words.* "Well, you know what I mean."

"I do," Babcock confirmed. "I have to ask you to take a different route to the park to preserve any evidence that may be intact." She pointed up the road toward a short pull off. "Back up and turn around there. We need to investigate this whole area."

"I'll show you," Oliver offered. "Follow me, ladies."

He hopped aboard his motorcycle while Penny and Nora climbed into the Peugeot. Penny gave Corky a few reassuring pats, and the dog settled down. Oliver drove to the other side of the turnaround point Babcock had indicated and waited for Nora. After some maneuvering, Nora redirected the car so they could take the alternate route.

"That was exciting," Nora said as they set off. "Poor Kenneth. I hope he'll be okay."

"Me too." Penny was thankful that they'd come across the man before dark. "Do you think we can check in on him later?"

"I'll ask Oliver," Nora said. "I'm sure he'll know what hospital they're taking Kenneth to."

The route took them through the heart of a village, where Penny spotted many references to the Lady of the Bog, including a restaurant, a bed and breakfast, a general store, and the museum, a fairly modern brick building.

"She really is an attraction," Penny said. "They certainly trade on her name."

"Who can blame them?" Nora asked. "It must be hard to make a living way out here."

Once through the settlement, Oliver navigated onto a side road labeled *Cillian's Bog Road*. "We found it from the other direction," Penny noted. The original route would have avoided the village.

"I'm going to study the map later," Nora said. "I like to have a good idea where I am and where I'm going."

After a short distance, Oliver signaled and steered down a rutted track. Another sign proclaimed that it was Gleason's Caravan Park. *Fit for Travelers* was the tagline. Despite that claim, the group of six or so caravans—which Penny had known in America as trailer homes—had all seen better days. Their paint and canopies were faded, the landscaping minimal. The one nice feature was the view. They were perched on a headland overlooking a smaller island and the ocean beyond.

"Nothing fancy," Oliver said as they climbed out of the Peugeot.

"But it's clean and cheap. I'll show you to yours." He watched as Nora opened the rear hatch. "Need help unloading?"

"Thanks," Nora said as she grabbed a suitcase. Corky whined dramatically. "Penny, can you get Corky?"

"Sure," Penny said. "I'll take him for a walk, then come back to help."

She opened the back door and clipped his leash on. As soon as his paws hit the ground, he tried to bolt.

"Hold on, Corky," she said, tightening her grip on the leash.

They headed toward the grassy headland, where Corky began to sniff and explore. Penny saw a tarp canopy sheltering a long table and a cooking station several yards away. A man and a woman stood beneath the canopy. By their body language, they appeared to be arguing. Penny shifted away to give them some privacy.

After Corky stretched his legs for ten minutes, Penny headed back toward the caravans to help Nora unload and get set up.

"We're in here, Penny." Nora stood on the steps of the caravan closest to the parking lot, so Penny veered in that direction.

Despite its compact size, the travel trailer had two bedrooms, a living room and kitchen combination, and a bathroom with a shower. One bedroom had a double bed, the other a set of bunk beds.

"Home away from home," Nora said, unpacking groceries. "You can choose your room."

"I'll take the one with bunks," Penny said. "Although he's welcome to the top bunk, I'm sure Corky would rather stay with you."

"That's settled, then." Nora opened the refrigerator and unloaded the contents of a small cooler. Although they would eat most of their meals with the group, they had brought some of their own supplies.

Oliver stepped into the caravan. A duffel strap was slung over one shoulder, and he held a sleeping bag and pillows in his arms. "Where do these go?"

Penny recognized her gear. "In the bunk room. Thank you, Oliver." He returned a few moments later. "Do you want to see the cooking setup and supplies, Penny? We're so glad to have your help."

"No problem." Penny smiled. "I enjoy cooking for a crowd." After she'd found out about the temporary job, she had begun collecting recipes for simple yet tasty and filling meals.

They left the caravan, Corky still on his leash, and crossed the grass to the canopy Penny had noticed earlier. No longer arguing, the man and woman were sitting at the table, both of them on their phones.

"Paige Matthews, Lee Cameron," Oliver said as they stepped under the tarp. "This is Nora, our new sketch artist, and Penny, her cousin. She's going to be cooking for us this week while Ralph is out. With help from everyone," he added.

With a toss of her dark braid, Paige shifted in her chair and studied Penny and Nora with narrowed eyes. She was probably in her midtwenties, lean and fit and attractive in an outdoorsy way. "Hello. Welcome aboard." She snapped her fingers at Corky. "Here, boy. Aren't you handsome?" He came closer and let her pet his head.

"Hey." Lee lifted a hand, barely glancing up from his screen. Even seated, Penny could tell he was tall and rangy, with a scruffy beard and long hair pulled back in a ponytail.

"Lee and Paige both teach with me," Oliver said.

"I'm still an adjunct." Paige lifted a travel cup and took a drink. "Someone practically has to die before they give out promotions at our university."

Lee snickered. "It's not that bad."

She shook a finger at him. "Easy for you to say, Mr. Professor."

Oliver rolled his eyes, and Penny got the sense that he spent a good deal of time smoothing ruffled feathers. "Listen up, both of you. I've got bad news."

"Our funding got cut?" Lee asked, brow creased.

"Kenneth is in the hospital," Oliver said. "He's had an accident."

Paige's complexion paled behind her tan. "Oh. Wow." She moved her hand back and forth. "Erase what I said about dying for a position, okay?"

Lee finally set down his phone and gave Oliver his full attention. "What happened?"

Oliver pulled out a chair and indicated that Nora and Penny should do the same. "It looks like he was hit by a car. These two found him."

Two pairs of suspicious eyes swiveled toward Penny and Nora. "You *found* him?" Lee asked.

"Yes," Nora said crisply. "He was lying in the road. We called an ambulance and the Garda, who checked out my car and confirmed that I didn't hit him."

"Of course," Lee muttered. "Is he going to be okay?"

"I hope so," Oliver said. "I'm going to call the hospital later and check on him."

"He woke up for a minute," Penny said. "He didn't say who hit him, though."

"Phew. That's good to hear. The waking-up part, I mean." Paige released a breath. "So, Oliver, are you in charge now?"

Oliver cocked one brow. "I suppose so. Unless they send someone else." He picked up his phone. "I suppose I'd better call the head of the department. They'll want an update." He rose from the chair. "Be right back."

Penny didn't feel like sitting awkwardly at the table with Paige and Lee, who were staring at their phone screens again. "Want to go for a walk, Nora?"

Corky let out a yip at the sound of one of his favorite words.

"Someone does." Nora got up. "Let's go. At least until Oliver's done with his call."

Lee and Paige didn't even seem to notice their departure. Once they were out of earshot, Penny said, "And I thought I was obsessed with my phone."

"No kidding." Nora let out the leash so Corky could run.

"Where is the dig, exactly?" Penny hadn't seen anything that resembled an archaeological site.

Nora pointed across the water. "See the island closest to us? It's over there."

Penny studied the landmass, which was a good distance offshore. "Are we using a boat to get there?"

"I hope so," Nora said. "I forgot my water wings."

"Guess I deserved that," Penny said with a laugh.

They strolled along the bluff while seagulls wheeled and squawked overhead. Below the cliff, waves splashed against a rocky headland, and then, farther along, a small white-sand beach.

"This is beautiful," Penny said as they followed the land's gentle slope down to the sand.

Corky was beside himself, prancing and whining in his eagerness to run along the open expanse. Seeing that no one else was nearby, Nora bent and unclipped the leash. He took off, cavorting along the packed sand closest to the water.

"I wish I had that much energy," Penny said. Despite her comment, she felt the stress and tiredness of the day drop away as they walked. The fresh sea air invigorated her.

"Uh-oh," Nora said. "I hope he behaves himself."

Penny followed Nora's gaze to Corky, who was introducing himself to a woman walking on the beach. She did a double take. "Is she wearing a cloak?"

Nora raised an eyebrow. "I think she might be."

The woman continued toward Nora and Penny, Corky trotting at her side. As she drew closer, Penny saw that she was dressed in garb similar to the Lady of the Bog, down to a metal breastplate over her chest and a circlet holding back her head of gray curls. She held a walking stick in one hand that she used to propel herself along.

"Local thespian?" Nora murmured.

"I hope so," Penny muttered back. She prepared to greet the woman pleasantly, despite her strange appearance, but didn't get a chance.

The woman lifted her stick high in the air. "Woe to those who interfere with sacred places," she declared ominously. "They shall be punished."

3

As Penny and Nora recoiled from her odd warning, the woman whirled around and began stomping across the sand, flailing with her stick as she dug into the soft surface. Even Corky appeared bewildered as he watched her go.

"That was certainly an unusual way to say hello," Nora said, pivoting to return to camp.

Penny followed her cousin, Corky bounding ahead of them. "I'll say. Any idea what she was talking about?"

"Judging by her outfit, I'd say she doesn't like the dig. It's a little too early for Halloween, so I can't chalk it up to that."

Penny chuckled. "I wonder if Oliver knows her. We'll have to ask."

They made it back to the caravan park without incident. Oliver had rejoined Lee and Paige, and they were all drinking tea.

"Kettle is still hot," Oliver said when they walked up.

"I'll get it." Penny went over to the cooking area and located a multi-burner gas grill set between stainless steel tables. Food lockers were laid out nearby alongside a refrigerator with a hasp and padlock, which hung open. She found a carton of milk inside the fridge. The tea bags waited in a tin beside an array of stained and battered mugs. She chose the two least grubby and draped tea bags in them.

At the table, Oliver was saying, "They're sending out another supervisor tomorrow."

"Who?" Paige sounded indignant. "Don't they think you can handle it?"

Oliver winced. "I'm sure it's not that. We need another person. And to answer your other question, they didn't tell me who."

"Great," Paige grumbled. "Anyway, I'm starving. When are we eating?"

Everyone faced Penny. "I'll start cooking right after I drink this tea." She had no idea what she was making since she hadn't investigated the food supplies yet.

"A decent meal at last," Lee said.

Paige glared at him. "I did my best."

"Hey, don't get all upset about it," he said. "I was including myself in that remark."

Penny handed Nora a mug and sat beside her at the table. "Before I take over meals, tell me—any dietary restrictions or special requests?" She braced herself in expectation for a variety of demands, but was pleasantly surprised when the three archaeologists glanced at each other with shrugs.

"To be honest, we'll all eat anything after a long day at the dig," Lee said. "We'll be grateful not to rely on takeaway from the restaurant."

Paige's lips curled. "Their food is so greasy. The real Lady of the Bog would not approve."

"Well, she might," Oliver said. "They had to eat a pretty high-calorie diet back then to keep warm in winter. Lots of animal fat."

The remark sparked a discussion about Iron Age diets. Celts from the period had grown wheat, other grains, and some vegetables. They had also raised cattle, sheep, and pigs.

"Very close to modern day," Penny said, surprised.

"No smoothies, though," Nora quipped.

Penny finished her tea and went to the food lockers to check the stock, unlocking them with a set of keys Oliver handed her. She found chicken cutlets and fresh vegetables in the refrigerator and rolls in the dry goods cupboard. "How about chicken burgers for dinner?"

she suggested. She spotted several ripe tomatoes in a bowl on top of the cabinet. "With a salad?"

"Sounds good to me," Oliver said. He swirled his mug before draining it. "I'm going to go do some paperwork."

The others wandered away as well, leaving Nora and Penny alone.

"Let's go get you some dinner, Corky." Nora whistled to her dog, who scrambled out from under the table. "Penny, I'll be right back to help."

"Take your time," Penny said, slicing a cucumber. After the meal, she would take an inventory and make a shopping list. She could already tell there wasn't enough food for the week.

Visions of easy yet delicious meals danced through her head. Beef stew. Chicken and dumplings. Spicy red lentil soup with tons of vegetables. Meat loaf and mashed potatoes. She could use the oven in their caravan for the meat loaf, as well as to heat dinner rolls.

Smiling, Penny began to hum as she chopped vegetables. She was going to enjoy her temporary cooking job.

After dinner, which was well received, Paige, Penny, and Nora lingered at the table. Oliver popped into his caravan, then emerged with his arms full of books and paperwork. He set it all down on the table, then spread out a map of Anoach Island and the smaller island, called Beag Anoach—literally translated as Little Anoach—along with a hand-drawn diagram of the dig.

"I thought you might like an overview of the project," he said. "Nora, these will help you to get up to speed." He patted the pile of materials, which contained several books and manila folders. "This is the background information we used to prepare for this project. Some of it, anyway."

Paige, who was reading at the table, gave a little snort of amusement. Lee had gone to his caravan to wash the dishes, an offer Penny appreciated.

"A little light reading, I see," Nora joked. "Actually, I'm very excited to learn more."

"So am I," Penny said. "I don't know much about the Iron Age. Well, beyond the Lady of the Bog's outfit."

"That reminds me," Nora said. "We ran into a very interesting woman on the beach. She was dressed in Lady of the Bog garb, and she made the most cryptic remark."

"'Woe to those who interfere with sacred places,'" Penny quoted. "'They shall be punished.'"

"So you've met Kinzi Eagan, our local eccentric." Paige rolled her eyes. "The woman is fully round the bend."

"I wouldn't say that," Oliver objected. "She's protective, and rightfully so. A lot of people don't understand or believe that we're not going to ruin or steal their heritage. Actually, what we do helps to preserve it. So many sites and artifacts are lost due to careless handling. Or thievery. So really, we're all on the same side."

"You can't tell her that," Paige said, returning to her book. "I've tried."

"That's all right. Our permits are all in order, and hopefully our work will speak for itself to her." Oliver smoothed the larger map, then beckoned to Penny and Nora. "Come take a look."

The two cousins listened as he pointed out the area on Beag Anoach where signs of an Iron Age settlement had been found.

"The activity in this area dates from around 400 BCE and was mentioned in writings from the twelfth century," Oliver explained. "Examining those documents led us to believe there was a settlement on Beag Anoach, a promontory fort right here." He indicated a headland. "Preliminary work confirmed this, so we set up a full-scale excavation."

He reached for one of the books and opened it to an illustration depicting a number of round buildings. "The early Celts lived in daub huts with thatched roofs called roundhouses set in some kind of enclosure of earth or stone. The one on Beag Anoach is stone."

"Tell them about the hoards," Paige said. "Not that they're why we do this."

Oliver smiled. "They aren't, but I've always dreamed of finding one, naturally. People are still discovering treasure from the Iron Age, usually gold or silver coins and jewelry. Recently, a bird-watcher stumbled upon a cache of gold coins from Boudica's reign. They were buried in a copper urn."

"Do you think we'll find a hoard here?" Nora asked, her eyes wide.

"It's possible," Oliver said. "The site has been undisturbed for over a thousand years, as far as we can tell." He put a finger to his lips. "We're not talking about it publicly, understand? We don't need to be swarmed by treasure hunters."

"So no social media posts about hoards, okay?" Paige added.

Penny was a little insulted, but bit her tongue.

Nora wasn't as restrained. "Got it," she said tartly. "Not that I would ever be so unprofessional."

Paige put up both hands. "Just saying. It's exciting stuff. Most people would be tempted to share."

"Not me," Nora said with a toss of her long curls. She shifted her attention back to Oliver. "Show us the work you've done so far."

On the diagram of the site, he pointed out where they were excavating the first roundhouse, which they suspected to be the largest one. "We're digging by hand and sifting the soil from each layer. It's a painstaking process."

Penny could imagine. It was hard enough digging a garden bed without worrying about what might be disrupted.

"Do you have sketches from the other artist?" Nora asked.

"They're digitized and on the server, which I'll give you access to." Oliver shuffled through his pile and withdrew a manila folder. "These are the hand drawings so far."

Penny peered over Nora's shoulder while she leafed through the drawings, which showed fragments of pottery, pieces of metal, and oddly broken stones.

"What are those?" Nora asked Oliver, indicating the rocks.

"Those are stones used to boil water," he said. "After being heated in a fire, they were put in a leather bag holding water. The shock would shatter the stones. At the same time, the water would heat up."

"How interesting." Penny marveled at the ingenuity of their ancestors. On the next page was a slab about six or eight inches long with a metal bowl at one end. "What is this?"

"It's a lamp," Oliver said. "They filled the bowl with tallow and lit it. The long piece is so they could carry it around."

Nora whistled. "One of the first candleholders. Amazing."

The next pages held a drawing of an ax-head and a bronze round mirror with a handle.

"This is pretty," Nora said, pointing to the mirror.

"A prized possession, we're guessing." Oliver's eyes sparkled with enthusiasm for the subject. "It's a real treat to find something like that, though we're thrilled when we come across any artifact. They help us learn more about these people from so long ago."

"I'm excited to see the dig," Penny said. "Thanks for including us."

"You're very welcome." Oliver rolled up the maps, then pulled out his phone. "I'm going to check in with the hospital and see how Kenneth is doing."

Penny pulled a small notebook out of her bag. "And I'm going to make a grocery list. Do I have to go off the island to shop?"

Oliver shook his head. "We have an account at the general store. If they don't have something you need, Mrs. Gleason will place an order and it will be here the next day."

"Do you want me to make breakfast and lunch?" she asked.

"If you want to," Oliver said. "We usually bring lunch with us to the island. Sandwiches and salads and the like."

"I can put out fixings," Penny said. "Let people design their own."

He gave her a thumbs-up and tapped his phone screen to connect the call to the hospital. He strolled off a short distance to talk.

Penny made a list of the meals she wanted to cook and started going through the lockers and refrigerator to see what they already had on hand.

A few moments later, Oliver came back. "Good news. He's going to be all right. Bad news, he'll be out of commission for a while with broken bones."

Paige cringed. "Poor guy."

Oliver sat down again. "I hope they catch the blighter who did it. How's it coming, Nora?"

"Very well, though it'll probably take me a while to go through all of this." Nora continued paging through books and papers. "Where do you keep the artifacts you find? Not at the dig site, I assume."

"They're locked up in Kenneth's caravan, inside a safe bolted to the floor, until someone from the lab picks them up. The landlady had a bit of a fuss about that, but she came around when Kenneth offered a hefty extra fee and a promise to fix the holes later."

"Makes sense," Nora said. "I bet they're attractive to thieves."

Oliver snapped his fingers. "Which reminds me that I need to get his keys. We can't get inside his caravan without them. I can't believe I nearly forgot that. I'm glad you said something, Nora." He gestured toward the trailer next to Penny and Nora's.

"Well, you weren't thinking about it." Nora flapped a dismissive hand. "We had more important concerns at the time."

"Who would like a cup of tea before bed?" Penny asked. Her plan was to take one back to the caravan and settle in. She hadn't even unpacked her sleeping bag and pillows yet, and after a long day, she was ready to relax.

Despite the caravan's age, it was clean and comfortable. Penny set up her bedroom and then took a shower, pleased that the water was hot with good pressure. Afterward, she curled up in her sleeping bag, pillows plumped, and grabbed her phone to call Finn.

"Hello, Penny," he said. "I was just about to ring. How is the island?"

She smiled at the evidence they were in sync. "Wonderful, except Nora and I almost ran over a man. Someone else hit him first."

A shocked silence met her statement. "You're pulling my leg," he finally said.

"I'm afraid not." Penny went on to detail the event. "Thankfully, he's going to be all right."

"Glad to hear that. How is the rest of it?"

"Gorgeous. Oh, let me tell you about the strange woman we met." Penny went on for a while, filling Finn in on the rest of her experience thus far. Once she'd run out of things to say, she asked, "So how's training?"

"Not as exciting as your day," he said ruefully. "Keep in touch, okay? I'll have my phone with me in case you need me."

You mean in case I run into even more trouble, as usual, she corrected him in her head. "Absolutely. Fingers crossed nothing else happens. I'm going to focus on making delicious meals and learning about the Iron Age."

A few minutes later, they hung up, and Penny sent him some pictures she'd taken of the park and the caravan. She read the paperback book she'd brought with her until her eyelids drooped and then switched out the light.

Corky's barking woke her. Penny's eyes popped open. All she could see was the red glow from the bedside alarm clock telling her it was one o'clock in the morning.

Her bedroom door burst open. Nora hovered in the doorway. "Penny, wake up," she said urgently. "I think someone is trying to break in next door."

4

Penny slid out of the sleeping bag as understanding dawned. "You mean Kenneth's place?"

"Yes." Nora gestured. "Come see."

Nora's bedroom overlooked the adjacent caravan, which was set at an angle to theirs. Hushing Corky, they peered out the window.

The other caravans all had small outside lights marking the entrance doors. Kenneth's was dark. Even so, Penny thought she saw someone. Putting a finger to her lips, she opened the window.

Distinct scraping sounds could be heard.

"That's it," Nora said. "I'm calling the Garda."

Penny put a hand on her arm. "What if it's Oliver or one of the others? They have a right to go inside."

"True, but why break in, at night, in the dark? Why not wait until morning and get in the right way?"

"You're right," Penny said. "Go ahead and call. Though it will probably take ages for them to get here."

Nora lowered the phone. "True. The prowler could be gone by then."

"Maybe call Oliver and let him decide?"

As they wavered in indecision, Corky nudged his way between them, pushing his snout right up to the screen. He let out a low, menacing growl followed by a deafening bark.

While Nora tried to settle him down, Penny peered out the window again. The person seemed to be gone, but she went out to the front steps to make sure.

"Corky, stay," Nora said, then joined Penny outside. "They took off?"

"Appears that way. Let's go check it out. We'll need your phone's flashlight." Penny's phone was still plugged in beside her bed, but she didn't want to waste time getting it.

Nora switched the light on and swung the beam across the front of the other caravan. No one was there.

Penny pointed to something shining dully in the grass. "What's that?"

Nora trotted down the stairs and across the grass. "It's a pry bar."

"So someone was trying to get in," Penny said when she reached Nora. She studied the tool's curved end, perfect to lever open a fairly flimsy door.

"I'm calling Oliver," Nora said. "He has to see this."

A yawning Oliver in plaid flannel pants and a T-shirt soon joined them, followed by Paige and Lee. Nora showed them the pry bar, then she and Penny shared the story.

"That's not mine," Lee said, crossing his arms.

"No one is accusing you," Paige told him.

With a sigh, Oliver ran his hand through his hair. "I guess I'd better call the Garda to report it. Get this incident on record, at least."

"Will they want to talk to us?" Paige asked, sounding disgruntled.

"Maybe," Oliver said. "We'd all better stay up, in case."

Penny knew a cue when she heard one. "I'll put the kettle on."

It was nearly three o'clock in the morning by the time the Garda left, taking the pry bar into evidence. They hadn't offered much insight beyond saying that caravan park break-ins weren't uncommon and to secure valuables in their vehicles.

Penny lay awake for a while, unable to settle her racing mind.

Perhaps break-ins were common, but she couldn't get past the fact that Kenneth's dwelling was where the dig's artifacts were being stored. Inside a safe bolted to the floor, but a thief wouldn't necessarily know that, even if they did somehow know about the artifacts. She believed that someone had found out about Kenneth's accident and was taking advantage.

The would-be thief could be anyone. She was pretty sure news of the hit-and-run was all over the island already. She lived in a small village and had witnessed the efficiency of a person-to-person gossip network. For all she knew, the Garda had broadcast a request for information related to the incident.

There wasn't much that she could do herself except keep her eyes open for any suspicious behavior. Thank goodness Corky was such a good watchdog.

Speaking of keeping her eyes open, she finally could not and slept.

"Wakey, wakey," Nora sang out.

Penny pried one eye open. "What time is it?" she croaked.

Both Nora and Corky had their heads around the door casing, which was cute.

"A little after eight." Nora grinned as Penny groaned. "No hurry, seriously. Oliver is frying some bacon and Paige made tea."

Despite Nora's words, Penny pushed herself upright, slightly embarrassed that she had slept in on her first morning. Breakfast wasn't on her list of duties, but she had wanted to make a good impression. "What's Lee doing?"

"Some kind of exercise routine out on the bluff." Nora gave a little snort. "Anyway, Oliver said we're not going out to the island today. They're sending the new supervisor, arrival time unknown, and we've been asked to cool our heels and wait."

Penny flopped back down. "Okay. Want to go to town later? I need to shop and put in a food order."

"Sounds good. Maybe we could go by the museum too."

"What a fascinating person the Lady of the Bog is," Penny mused.

"You'll get to see her," Nora said. "They have her on display at the museum."

Penny closed her eyes at the image that presented itself.

"Oliver says it's really not gruesome," Nora continued.

"We'll see." Penny popped up again. "I'll get dressed. After our middle-of-the-night adventure, I'm ready for breakfast."

Nora and Corky exited and a moment later, Penny heard the front door open and close. She slid out of bed, eager to begin the day even if she was still a little groggy.

"Scrambled eggs?" Oliver greeted Penny as she joined the others under the canopy. Lee, Nora, and Paige were already digging in, Corky waiting hopefully for stray tidbits.

"I'd love some, thanks." Penny put a tea bag in a mug and added hot water, then sat down beside Nora. "Sorry I overslept."

"No worries. It was a crazy night, and I enjoy cooking occasionally." Oliver spooned eggs onto a plate. "The new supervisor is going to arrive at some point, probably late afternoon. We can get caught up on paperwork and arrange for a pickup of the artifacts after I get Kenneth's caravan unlocked."

"Not a bad idea, boss," Lee said. "Don't want a repeat of last night."

"Good thing Nora brought her dog," Oliver said. "He saved the day. Didn't you, boy?" Corky whined and wagged his tail at the attention.

"Nora and I are going into town to grocery shop and explore," Penny announced. "If anyone has any special requests, let me know."

Lee's eyes lit up. "Can you buy some McVitie's chocolate-covered digestive biscuits? I love those with a cuppa in the afternoon."

"I certainly can," Penny said. The wheat rounds were crumbly and delicious with the perfect amount of chocolate.

"If you're taking orders, I'd like some bottled iced teas," Paige said. "They're a nice change from water all the time."

"Can do," Penny replied. Oliver set the plate in front of her, and she added several pieces of bacon from a platter plus a slice of whole wheat toast, already buttered. He'd added cheese and finely diced onions to the eggs, and they were delicious.

"Aren't they good?" Nora smiled. "Oliver used to make the best meals when we were in school. Using the cheapest ingredients."

"Maybe I should consult you about the menu," Penny said as Oliver joined them at the table.

Oliver chuckled, unrolling a napkin containing silverware. "I gravitate toward ham sandwiches and ramen noodles nowadays."

Paige scooped up the last of her eggs. "You two met at school? I was wondering."

"We were neighbors," Nora clarified before relaying the details of how they had become close friends.

An hour later, with Corky along for the ride, they drove down to the village. "Store first and then the museum?" Nora asked. "It's cool enough out that we can leave the groceries in the car for a while. Or maybe we can get our order together and then pick it up later."

"That makes sense. Get the work out of the way, then we can take our time checking out the exhibits." Penny opened her notebook and reviewed her list. She'd make that night's dinner from what they currently had available and order ingredients for the rest of the week.

A few minutes later, they parked outside Gleason's General Store, a squat brown building with a weathered front porch and very little in the way of decoration. Nora entered first, followed by Penny, who let the screen door close too fast. It twanged shut with a thump.

"Sorry," Penny said with a sheepish smile as the plump woman seated behind the counter glanced over.

The woman, who had a head of red curls and a broad, freckled face, didn't return the smile. "Help you?" she asked.

"I hope so." Wood floor creaking noisily underfoot, Penny approached the counter, list in hand. "I'm here to order food for the Beag Anoach dig. A week's worth for six people."

Nora began to browse the crowded shelves, which included everything from food to household goods to sporting supplies and tools. It was a true general store.

"We can do that," the woman said, perking up a little. "You're staying in my caravan park. I'm Muriel Gleason."

"Pleased to meet you. I'm Penny Cavanagh, and that's my cousin, Nora Murphy."

A man strolled in from the back. He was medium height and lean, wearing faded jeans and T-shirt, work boots, and a ball cap. He came to stand behind the counter, watching without saying a word.

Penny threw him a smile before turning back to Muriel. "Shall we go through my list? We'll take anything you have in stock today, and the rest we'd like to order."

When they were halfway through collecting the items, Muriel sighed. "It's a shame about Kenneth, isn't it?"

For a moment, Penny worried that Kenneth's condition had worsened overnight. "What do you mean?"

"Hit by a car, he was." Muriel's eyes narrowed. "I understand you and the other one were on the scene right after."

"We were," Penny said. "But the way you put it made me worry that he'd gotten worse."

The young man behind the counter laughed. "Don't mind Ma. She likes to wind people up."

"Away with you, Carroll," Muriel ordered. "Aren't you taking the group out to Beag today?"

He shifted his stance against the wall to a more comfortable one. "Not today, Ma. They're hanging around the park."

"Well, get over there and mow the grass then," Muriel barked. "It grows like crazy this time of year."

With a sigh, Carroll adjusted his hat and pulled away from the wall. "I'll go after lunch."

Soon, Muriel had rung up the day's purchases and the order that would come in by the next morning. The dig had a charge account as Oliver had said, so it was a simple matter of Penny signing for the purchases. She arranged to swing back by later to pick up the food they'd bought so the perishables would stay cold.

"Where are you headed next?" Muriel asked.

Sensing she was providing grist for the storekeeper's gossip mill, Penny told her, "We're going to the museum to see the Lady."

Muriel nodded. "She's worthy of it. Made this whole town, she did."

With that endorsement, Penny and Nora drove to the museum, which was a few blocks away. They could have walked, but they decided to save that pleasure for another day. Penny spotted an ice cream kiosk and a couple of gift shops on the way and thought it would be fun to meander through the village on foot sometime.

As Penny had noticed before, the museum was in a fairly modern, one-story building with a decent-size parking lot. A concrete sidewalk led to the double-doored entrance, and a huge vertical window took up much of the rest of the front.

Before going inside, they walked Corky around the block, then left him in the car with all the windows open and a bowl of water. He watched forlornly as they walked away and Nora called back, "We won't be long. Promise."

Inside the front doors, the women entered a lobby with polished floors and a small coatroom to one side. Straight ahead, an older man stood behind a visitor desk with a waist-high counter. He was bulky in build, with thinning hair and large features.

"Good morning, ladies," he said, his voice booming out in the quiet lobby. "Welcome to Lady of the Bog Museum. Your first time here?"

"It is," Nora said as they approached the desk. "We're working with the dig on Beag Anoach."

He brightened. "You are? How fascinating." He held out a meaty hand. "I'm Barry Danvers, the museum director." Rocking on his heels slightly, he added, "My ancestor, Dr. Horace Danvers, found the Lady."

Nora shook his hand, introducing herself and Penny. "We're interested in learning all we can before we start work."

"We arrived yesterday," Penny said, shaking Barry's hand as well. "From Blarney Green, in County Cork."

"Near the castle? Nice area." Barry gestured to an array of printed materials in a slotted display on the desk front. "We've got museum maps and other publications detailing some of the finds." A phone on the counter rang shrilly. "Please let me know if you have any questions."

Barry answered the phone, then went into a private office to talk, the door open to the lobby. Nora and Penny browsed the rack and selected a few brochures.

"Shall we make a circuit?" Nora asked, opening the map.

"Sure." Penny saw that the museum exhibits were located on both sides and behind the lobby area. Next to a gift kiosk stocked with mugs, ornaments, magnets, and the like, they spotted a sign that read *Enter Here*.

On the way into the exhibits, Penny paused at the kiosk. "More Lady of the Bog items. I might buy a few for the gang back home."

"I think I'll get a souvenir for myself too," Nora said.

Inside the museum exhibit room, panoramic displays illustrated various facets of life and history on the island. To Penny's delight, one life-size diorama showed an Iron Age dwelling with a small family at work. The woman hovered over a fire while a child threw grain to chickens and a man used a crude plow in a nearby field. Penny and Nora spent quite some time there taking in every detail.

"This is really going to help me put the finds in context," Nora said.

"It's so interesting," Penny mused. "The world has changed so much in many ways, but we still have the same requirements for living. Food, shelter, family."

"From what little I've read so far, some of the jewelry and other items they've found show high levels of artistry." Nora gave a little snort. "As you might expect, the archaeologists are amazed. Even they tend to think past civilization wasn't nearly as sophisticated as us."

"Not Oliver, I hope?" Penny said, thinking Nora's friend seemed more open-minded than that. They moved along to a panorama depicting island ocean and shore life featuring fish, shellfish, and mammals.

"He's different," Nora said. "Really great. I wonder why they don't make him the supervisor."

"It's probably political," Penny said. "Isn't that always the way?"

"True." Nora studied the display. "See the humpback whales and basking sharks? Maybe we'll see those when we're out in the boat."

"I've never heard of basking sharks." Penny read the information card, translating meters to feet in her head. "Over twenty feet long? Wow. Good thing they're harmless." Basking sharks ate plankton that they filtered through their huge teeth.

Penny's steps slowed when they reached the glass case holding the Lady of the Bog, readily identified by a huge sign on the wall. The area also featured another diorama depicting her when alive, standing on the edge of a peat bog amid hummocks of grass and small pools of water.

Nora inhaled deeply as she surveyed the preserved remains. "This is amazing. Her clothes, her hair, even her shoes."

Penny took in the clothing fragments first, seeing that the woman had been wearing a sheepskin cloak and a wool skirt. The depictions had taken some license, showing the Lady in summer garb. The shoes were the same, though—leather ankle boots with a pierced design. Penny thought they were surprisingly attractive.

Finally, she stole a glimpse at the mummy. A body lay on its back, intact although with bronze-colored leathery skin from the tannins in the bog, according to the sign. Her hair was also tinted a reddish color.

Penny was awed. "She's incredible. Isn't it neat to think that she's still remembered over two thousand years after her death?"

"Someone like her was our ancestor," Nora said. "Similar groups lived around what is now Blarney Green."

Penny hadn't quite made that connection, and it was stunning. She immediately felt protective of the Lady, beginning to understand the fascination she held for people like Kinzi Eagan. "Too bad there aren't written records," she said. "We might be able to find out exactly who her descendants are."

"No one has found anything but some stone writing called ogham inscriptions, and those are from centuries after the Iron Age. Personally, I have a hard time believing the Celts were illiterate at the same time much of the world had written languages, like Greek, Hebrew, Latin, and Chinese."

"That would be an exciting discovery." Penny laughed. "Listen to me. I've been bitten by the archaeology bug."

Realizing they should get back to Corky and pick up the groceries, Penny and Nora decided to leave the rest of the exhibits for another time.

On the way out, Barry flagged them down. "What do you think of our little museum?"

"I love it," Penny said. "You've done a beautiful job on the displays."

Barry puffed up with pride. "It is quite a gem for such a small facility, I always think. Thanks to our generous donors and sponsors, that is." He held out a small pamphlet. "If you'd like to read more about the discovery of the Lady, this is a good start."

"I would." Nora took the pamphlet and tucked it into her purse. "Thank you."

Barry edged closer, lowering his voice although they were still alone. "Is there any news concerning Kenneth McCarty? I understand he met with an accident yesterday."

That's one way of putting it. "As far as we know, he's fine," Penny said. "Still in the hospital, but I'm sure he'll heal. Oliver from the dig checked in on him this morning."

Barry's shoulders visibly relaxed. "That is so good to hear. I've met Kenneth and consider him a friend."

"I think he's allowed visitors," Penny said. "On another topic, I was thinking it's too bad we don't know more about the Lady. To trace her descendants, I mean."

"No parish records existed at that time," Barry said. "Or even gravestones. I'm afraid it's a dead end."

"What about DNA?" Penny asked. "Surely that might provide information."

The director frowned. "That would be very expensive, if you could even get DNA after a couple thousand years soaking up acid in a bog. Plus, we don't like to disturb the Lady. We can't imagine damaging her after she's been so well-preserved for so long."

"It was just a thought," Penny said hastily. "I understand." What she understood was that Barry was very protective of the mummy.

"Before you go." He held out slips of paper. "These are coupons for my bed-and-breakfast and restaurant. I hope you take advantage of them while you're here."

Penny glanced at the coupons. Unsurprisingly, both enterprises referenced the Lady of the Bog in their names. "Thank you, Barry. We're staying at the caravan park, but maybe we'll eat at the restaurant sometime."

"Pass on whatever you don't use," Barry said. "And please feel free to come back anytime."

"Will do," Nora said.

Penny waved. "Have a good day."

Once they were outside, Nora blew out a breath. "These people here aren't merely proud. They're obsessed."

"The Lady is practically the basis of their economy, so I get why," Penny said.

They picked up the groceries, which Carroll loaded in the car with a grumble, and headed back to the caravan park.

Nora eased the Peugeot down the drive. As they approached the caravans, she gasped. "I don't believe it."

"What?" All Penny saw was Oliver standing with a blonde woman near Kenneth's caravan. Both had their arms crossed.

"That's Caroline, Oliver's ex-wife," Nora said, her eyes narrowing. "What is she doing here?"

5

As they parked and climbed out of the car, Penny wondered fleetingly if Caroline had come to reconcile with Oliver. Something about their body language said otherwise, though.

Nora let Corky out. "Let's ask Oliver to help with the food so he can get away from her."

With the dog running ahead, nose down to the grass, the pair approached. As they got there, Caroline was saying, "You seem annoyed, Oliver."

"I am," he said. "Not with you specifically. Why didn't they bump me up to supervisor? I did most of the legwork on this project."

Arms still crossed, Caroline rolled her eyes. "You know how the department works. Besides, I have tons of relevant experience to offer." That sounded conciliatory until she added, "So, buck up. This is the way it is."

"Hello." Nora waved as they got closer. "How nice to see you, Caroline." Penny could tell Nora was being polite.

Caroline reared back. "Nora? Oh my, it has been an age." In contrast to Nora's tepid greeting, she ran at Nora and gave her a big hug. "What are you doing here?"

"Don't you know, *leader*?" Oliver sniped under his breath.

Nora either didn't hear him or pretended not to. "I'm filling in for the dig artist who's on medical leave." She gestured to Penny. "Meet my lovely cousin, Penny. She's also filling in to make meals, which is fortunate for us."

Penny waved. "Nice to meet you."

Nora pivoted to Oliver. "We have quite a few groceries in the car. Could you help us unload, please?" She whistled to Corky, who was running around a short distance away. "Stay with me, boy."

"Right away." He marched toward Nora's vehicle.

Caroline pulled out a set of keys. "I'm staying in this caravan. Kenneth won't be back, so he gave me his keys when I stopped by to visit him." She climbed the stairs and unlocked the door.

Penny hurried after Nora and Oliver, who were already at the Peugeot, grabbing bags and a box of food while Corky watched in interest.

Between the three of them, they were able to carry everything to the dining area in one trip. They set it all on the table, then unloaded items into the refrigerator and lockboxes.

"So, Oliver," Nora said as they worked. "They put Caroline in charge?"

Oliver grunted. "Yep. I couldn't believe my eyes when she pulled up and said she was taking over for Kenneth." He folded a paper grocery bag with firm movements. "Later, after I cool down, I'm going to call the head of the department. He's fully aware of our history. Talk about adding insult to injury." Hurt flashed in his eyes.

Nora touched his arm. "We get it. Anyone would be upset. Be careful, though. Don't let your feelings about Caroline interfere. This dig is your baby."

"You're right," Oliver said with a sigh. "Before I talk to the head, I'll write a report detailing my work so far. Supervisors tend to take credit, which I can't allow to happen. Then I'll start putting out feelers for a new position. Enough is enough."

Penny found herself getting angry on Oliver's behalf. Would Caroline really swoop in and take credit for his work? Then she reined in her thoughts. That might be Oliver's anxieties speaking. She needed to keep an open mind about Caroline since she had to work with her too.

One way or another, she expected that spending time around the exes would be anything but boring.

After getting up to speed about the dig, Caroline decided they should spend the afternoon on Beag Anoach. Penny packed a picnic lunch, and they all went down to the caravan park's dock, where Carroll waited with a motorboat.

They climbed aboard, Carroll helping with the food coolers, and set off across the sparkling bay, the boat gently bouncing on the waves.

Penny tilted her head back to gaze at the deep-blue sky, with a few clouds massed behind the mountains and far off at sea. "What a beautiful afternoon," she said to Nora, who was seated beside her on the bench. Corky sat on the deck, leaning against Nora's knees.

The journey didn't take long. Soon, they docked at the smaller island, with Carroll tying the boat to a post. After Caroline arranged a pickup time with him, the party of archaeologists donned their backpacks and wheeled the coolers and a tool carrier along the beach.

"The dig is over there." Oliver pointed to a headland off to their left. "It'd be nice if we could dock closer, but the shore is all rocks on that side."

"We should bring over an all-terrain vehicle or a golf cart," Lee said. "That would make it a lot easier to get around and move the artifacts if we find more."

"Not a bad idea," Caroline said. "Give me a few days to get settled, and I'll check into it."

Lee, who was pulling the tools, smiled with satisfaction, throwing Oliver a triumphant smile. "Glad someone agrees with me."

"It was Kenneth who put the kibosh on it the first time," Oliver said. Then he seemed to hear the defensiveness in his voice and clamped his mouth shut with a frown.

Caroline strode ahead of everyone else, shoulders square and head high. Penny could tell she was a take-charge kind of person.

Oliver halted on a small rise with a view of the headland below. "Can you see the village?" he asked Penny and Nora.

While the rest went ahead, the cousins peered at the site, Oliver watching them. At first, Penny could only see humps and hollows interrupted by furrows dug into the soil. Small white canopies dotted the area, likely for shelter from the sun.

At last, the shapes coalesced. "I see it," she said. "The ring around and then the buildings inside." These features were mere suggestions, but once she saw them, she couldn't *not* see them.

Oliver grinned. "When you fly overhead, it's really clear. Some sites you don't find until you dig something up. Often there are buildings from different eras in layers on top. This one was abandoned and nothing else was built over it. It's covered with layers of soil and plants."

They continued down the hill to the official dig area. Caroline made a circuit with Lee, stopping to peer into pits or trenches. Paige unpacked tools, a ball cap on her head and her hair in a ponytail. Like the others, she wore a light, long-sleeved shirt and loose trousers for protection from the sun.

"That's where we usually eat," Oliver said, pointing out a canopy to one side. "You can park the coolers under there and help for a while if you'd like."

"I'd love to," Penny said, eager to be part of the crew instead of merely watch.

Nora helped Penny haul the food, and then they and the dog strolled over to Paige, who was inside a trench sheltered partially by a tarp.

"Do you want to help dig, Nora? Penny, you can sift." Paige handed Nora a trowel. "If we find something in situ, you can stop and sketch."

Finding that plan agreeable, they got to work. Corky sprawled on a patch of grass supervising. Even if she found nothing but pebbles and a stray twig or two, Penny found it relaxing to sift. She appreciated the repetition of dumping buckets of soil onto a screen and pushing it gently through.

She was thinking about stopping for lunch when she saw a man walking over the small hill toward them. Corky leaped up to bark, subsiding at Nora's instruction.

Penny recognized the man as he got closer. "It's Barry Danvers. I wonder what he wants."

Paige sniffed. "Probably has some new issue with us. He's been a royal pain since we started."

"You'd think he'd be excited about the dig," Nora said. "You might find new artifacts for his museum. Which was quite well done, I thought."

"It's very nice," Paige agreed. "I think it's more of a control issue. He's afraid something to do with the Lady will slip through his fingers. Since his ancestor found her, he seems to think she belongs to his family personally. Who knows? She might have lived in this settlement even if she was found in the bog on Anoach."

There was probably almost no way to prove that, but Penny could see why the thought would be attractive. She wondered if they might even build replica houses near the dig site at some point once the work was complete. An Iron Age village would be a fantastic attraction and learning tool.

They continued working, watching as Barry made his way straight to Caroline, who was conferring with Lee and Oliver nearby. His voice clearly carried on the slight breeze. "Are you Caroline Pierce?" he asked.

Caroline's shoulders went back. "I am. And you are?"

"Barry Danvers. I run the local museum where the Lady of the Bog is exhibited."

"You're the man who is stonewalling me," Caroline said. "I got your reply this morning."

"What did you contact Barry about?" Oliver asked, his tone testy.

"I want to do strontium testing on the Lady's hair," Caroline replied, her tone casual.

"It's a specialized analysis," Paige murmured to Nora and Penny. "You can identify all kinds of information from hair."

Barry's hands fisted at his side. "I forbid it. The Lady is not to be disturbed."

"What?" Caroline laughed, a pealing sound that rang out across the field. "How absurd. We're talking one hair here." She put up her forefinger. "One. Hair. We'll be able to learn so much from that. It will more than pay for itself with its addition to our knowledge of this area during that time period, to say nothing of how it will boost her value to the local economy. I'm mainly interested in her diet and nutrition. We're lucky to have that opportunity."

"You don't. Have the opportunity, I mean." Barry sounded like he was gritting his teeth. "You aren't the first to ask for X-rays and examinations and analysis. My board agrees that the answer is no."

Caroline smiled. "Thanks for your thoughts, Barry. I really appreciate your coming here to deliver them in person. I'll probably talk to your board myself, okay? They'll enjoy hearing about all the grants and support I can find for your little museum. I'm sure you need more money. We all do."

"Wow," Paige said, still under her breath. "She really knows how to ruffle feathers."

Barry began to splutter, his face flushing deep red. "You'll regret this. I can promise you that much." With a final huff, he marched away, storming past Penny without even a glance. She was grateful he didn't notice her, in case his wrath spilled over.

"That wasn't smart, Caroline," Oliver said once Barry was over the rise. "He could try to get our permits revoked."

Caroline snorted. "Good luck with that. He doesn't have as much power as he thinks. We're solid. Take my word for it. Let's get to work."

"I hope she's right," Paige said as the entire team resumed digging. "If he makes a big enough fuss, we could have some trouble."

"When I met him, I immediately got the impression that he's protective of the Lady," Penny said.

"'The Lady is not to be disturbed.'" Nora repeated Barry's words dramatically, making them all laugh. "Seriously, though. He really is taking it all a bit far."

Penny checked the time. "Shall we have lunch? I could use the energy boost."

Nora and Paige agreed they were hungry, so they went to the dining canopy to eat while the other three kept working.

"We don't stand on ceremony while working," Paige said. "Eat when you're hungry, rest when you're tired. As long as you're productive."

Penny couldn't find fault with the group's work ethic. After the meal, they plugged away for a few more hours, digging and sifting. One pottery shard was found, which Nora drew and Oliver photographed.

"I'm about ready to call it a day," Paige said. Her clothing, gloves, and face were covered with a fine coating of dust. She sighed as she dumped a shovelful of soil onto the pile. "Some days are like this. No progress at all. In fact, most days are like this."

Penny could see her point. She blanched at the thought of examining every square inch of ground that was considered part of the site. Patience was definitely required in such an occupation.

She plopped another heap of soil onto the sifter and began shaking it. Halfway through, something began to bounce. She kept sifting, thinking it was a flat rock. Her heart began to beat faster as a wild thought took hold. Taking off a glove, she picked up the object, which was about an inch in diameter, and began to rub it gently.

The gleam of gold shined through.

6

Penny yelped.

"What's up?" Nora asked.

"This." Penny held out the disc. "I think it's a coin. It's flat, it's gold—"

"Gold?" Paige climbed out of the trench. "Let me see." She reached out her hand and Penny dropped the piece into her palm. Paige found a soft brush and began to sweep away the remaining dirt. "You're right. It is a coin. Nora, hand me that box."

Nora grabbed a nearby box that had been set out to collect discovered artifacts.

Paige placed the coin inside and then stood, cupping her hands around her mouth. "Hey, Oliver. Important find."

Oliver, Lee, and Caroline climbed out of their trench, Caroline frowning. Was it because Paige had called Oliver over instead of Caroline, the official supervisor? A not-so-subtle dig, Penny thought.

When the trio arrived, Caroline shouldered her way to the front. "What do you have?"

Paige handed Penny the box. "It's your find, Penny."

Feeling flustered all of a sudden, Penny held the box out. "I was sifting when I found this." The coin, although dull, gleamed in the sunlight.

The others exchanged glances, and Oliver cleared his throat. "May I?" he asked. At Caroline's nod, he pulled out a magnifying loupe and studied the coin. "It's a gold stater. A Celtic coin. The original staters were Greek and made of silver."

"You know what that means?" Lee put a hand on Oliver's arm. "There might be a hoard here."

"One coin does not a hoard make," Caroline said in a quelling tone.

"It's more than we had yesterday," Paige said. "Good work, Penny."

Penny's cheeks warmed at the attention. "All I did was sift."

"Document and label it right away," Caroline said. "We'll have to get that to the lab ASAP for authentication. Good work, team." Her bare smile encompassed Nora and Paige as well as Penny. She touched her stomach. "Is there food? I'm famished."

"I'll show you," Penny said, taking off her other glove. "Come with me."

Leaving Nora and Paige to carry on, Penny helped the others select sandwiches, chips, and cold drinks.

"This is good," Lee said, tearing into his sandwich. "Thanks, Penny."

Oliver and Caroline echoed Lee's thanks, then Oliver said, "I think we should concentrate our efforts in that area. See if there are more staters."

"Perhaps." Caroline took a dainty bite, chewing thoughtfully. "It could be a stray, though. Why don't I join Paige, and you two keep going with the second trench?"

Oliver started to object, then clamped his mouth shut.

Lee had no such qualms. "How about this?" he countered, his tone belligerent. "We all dig in that area until we're satisfied it was a one-off. We should all be in on the discovery."

Penny could see the fairness and efficiency of Lee's plan. A focused effort by the whole team would be much more likely to quickly reveal whether or not there was more gold.

Caroline shook her head. "Let's keep it the way I said. I'm sure there are important discoveries in the second trench too. It was a reasoned choice to dig there, was it not?"

Even Penny felt the sting of that remark. Oliver couldn't argue without denigrating his own decision. She felt a pang of sympathy for Nora's friend. Caroline was a very challenging person to deal with. That she was Oliver's ex added serious insult to injury.

Caroline kept them working late, and the sun was lowering in the sky when Carroll returned to pick them up. Although Penny was dirty, tired, and starving, a hum of excitement buoyed her spirits.

They had found treasure, even if it was a lone coin. Judging by their chatter and barely suppressed excitement, the archaeologists were hopeful about discovering more. Not only was such a find notable, continued funding was sure to follow as Beag Anoach's importance was elevated.

Once on shore, they unloaded and carted everything up to the caravan park. Lee began grumbling about the need for a golf cart on the main island too. Penny, who was pulling a wheeled cooler over hills and uneven terrain, secretly agreed. She was going to be in very good shape by the time she left the dig.

"No rush with dinner," Caroline said when they reached the caravans. She glanced at her sports watch. "Does an hour work?"

"Sure. I'll put out cheese and crackers and other snacks to tide everyone over." Penny made a mental note to cube cheese and cut up vegetables in advance for upcoming days.

"You're a woman after my own heart," Lee said. "I'm absolutely famished."

Everyone dispersed to clean up and rest. Penny and Nora dropped off the coolers and went to their caravan to shower.

As Nora bent to feed Corky, she groaned. "Every muscle hurts," she said, rubbing one shoulder. "You can go first since you have food duty. After I shower, I'll come help."

"I'm keeping it easy with spaghetti and meatballs tonight," Penny told her cousin. "Your main job will be keeping me company."

Nora grinned. "That I can do."

After Penny's shower, she took a few moments to text Finn before walking over to the dining area. *We had a very exciting day. Big discovery.* Then she had second thoughts. Finn was completely trustworthy, but she didn't want to be the source of any accidental leaks. Caroline and Oliver needed complete control of what was said and when. *Just realized I can't tell you about it*, she added.

His answer came straight back. *That's OK. I understand. Otherwise, how is it?*

Hold on. I'll call you. She dialed Finn, first telling him what she was doing.

"Spaghetti dinner sounds great," Finn said. "The food here—well, suffice it to say it's not exactly exceptional."

"That's too bad," Penny sympathized. "You already ate tonight?"

"A while ago. I'm studying in my room. There is a ton of material to work through."

Penny retrieved the meatballs from the caravan freezer, then headed outside. "We worked late tonight. The new supervisor arrived today, and she wanted to make up for lost time."

"Understandable."

She lowered her voice, mindful that others might overhear. "Get this. It's Oliver's ex-wife. That's who they sent. Can you believe that?"

Finn groaned. "Careless of them."

"Very," Penny agreed. "She's not particularly easy to deal with for any of us. On the plus side, she's dedicated and driven. Competent, from what I can tell."

Once under the dining canopy, Penny combined the meatballs and sauce in a pot on the stove, then left it to simmer while she made the appetizers. She put the phone on speaker and propped it against a lantern.

Then she had a bright idea. "Why don't we switch to a video call?"

"Great thinking," Finn agreed.

Penny changed the settings and put the phone back, showing her prepping food on his end. On her end, all she could see was his handsome face—not that she minded in the least.

After Penny cut up enough cheese and vegetables, she placed them on a platter along with crackers and dip, then took Finn on a video tour of the caravan park and down to the bluff. She filled him in on her day while they went—the trip to town, the museum, the dig. The Lady of the Bog.

Finn's brows rose suddenly. "What's that creature behind you? The four-legged one, I mean."

Penny glanced behind to see Nora and Corky taking a walk. She waved them over to say hello. Corky, who was quite fond of Finn, tried to lick the phone, which made them laugh.

Over at the dining area, Oliver and Lee were gathered around the table. Caroline and Paige were on their way there.

"I'd better go boil water for noodles," Penny said reluctantly. "Talk soon?"

"Tomorrow," Finn promised. "This time of day works best for me. They have us busy from dawn until dinner." He blew a kiss into the phone. "Stay out of trouble."

Penny blew a kiss back. "That happens to be a talent of mine."

He was still laughing when she hung up.

The next morning, Penny was cracking eggs into a bowl when Oliver wandered up, the first to appear. "Water's hot if you want a cup of tea," she told him as she picked up a whisk and began to beat the eggs.

Oliver opened a tea bag and placed it in a mug. "Have you seen Caroline?"

"Not yet. You're the first." Even Nora was still lazing around inside their caravan, playing with Corky. Penny shifted back to the stove, where she flipped the sausage links.

"I went by her caravan and she wasn't there." Oliver tilted the kettle and filled his mug.

"Maybe she's out for a walk." Penny continued to beat the eggs. She wouldn't cook them until more people showed up, she decided. "When are we going to the site?"

Oliver added a splash of milk to his tea. "Around midday. I was thinking of visiting Kenneth at the hospital this morning. Want to go?"

"I'm in. Nora probably will be too. He doesn't know us, but I do feel a slight responsibility for him after we found him."

Paige and Lee joined them, but neither had seen Caroline. Penny prepared the batch of scrambled eggs, figuring she could make Caroline's breakfast to order when she showed up.

An hour later, Penny was strategizing lunch when Oliver returned to the dining area, mug in hand. Paige and Lee had returned to their caravans, and Nora was painting on a small canvas down by the bluff, Corky at her feet.

"Still haven't seen Caroline?" he asked.

Penny felt a pang of concern. "Should we start worrying?" If Caroline had left before breakfast, she had been gone a couple of hours.

"Maybe," Oliver said, making a fresh cup of tea. "She can't have gone far. She does like her long walks, though, come to think of it."

"Are we still going to the hospital to visit Kenneth?" Penny asked. "We can go before I have to make lunch."

"I'd like to," Oliver said. "I feel rather remiss not going before now."

"Me too." Remembering the moment when she and Nora had come across him lying in the road still made Penny shiver. Their intervention had likely saved his life.

"Do you want Nora and me to go down to the beach and search for Caroline?" Penny suggested. "We can take Corky for a walk." She hoped they would find Caroline—and not the eccentric Kinzi Eagan.

"If you want," Oliver said. "I'll hold down the fort here. And when she does show up, she can wait for us to get back from the hospital before we go to the island." His tone was acerbic. "We owe Kenneth that much."

Penny agreed but didn't say so. The last thing she wanted to do was fan the flames between Caroline and Oliver, or between any members of the party for that matter. She was in the unfortunate position of observing without the ability to smooth things over.

"I'll go talk to Nora, then," Penny said. "We'll be back within the hour."

Nora was amenable to taking a walk on the beach. She packed up her painting supplies, but left them where they were and grabbed Corky's leash.

Following the same route as they had previously, they strolled along the cliffs and then down to the sandy beach. Penny groaned when she saw the empty expanse of sand. "Where can she be?"

Nora frowned. "It is really starting to seem strange. Yes, Caroline is incredibly independent. However, she wouldn't be so irresponsible as to leave everyone dangling. I'm sure this dig is hugely important to her."

"What should we do?" Penny asked, worry beginning to knot in her chest. "Can you think of anywhere else we should check?"

Nora pointed toward the headland. "Maybe over in that rocky area. She might have fallen and hurt her ankle or something."

Penny checked the tide. It was out far enough that they could skirt the cliffs, but she could tell it was on the turn. "Okay. We'd better hurry, though."

Nora studied the waves. "Agreed. I'd hate to try to climb the cliff."

"Seriously." Penny shuddered, imagining the three of them trapped by the water. "I'm not exactly a rock climber."

They skirted an outcropping of rocks, the sand underfoot still damp from the water that had receded a couple of yards. Creamy waves curled, the foam creeping closer with every breaker. The air was even brinier, and Penny saw tide pools she'd love to explore under other circumstances.

To their left, the bluff rose in a series of jumbled stones, with a sheer cliff right under where Nora had been painting. After they clambered over a couple of big boulders, the slabs below the cliff came into view.

Caroline's body lay sprawled on the rocky ledge, blonde hair fluttering in the breeze and limbs at an unnatural angle.

For a moment, Penny's brain refused to make sense of what she was seeing. Then the truth became all too clear.

Caroline was dead.

7

Her face pale as milk, Nora stood frozen while Corky whined and strained at the leash. "She's been lying here the whole time?"

"No one would have heard her when she fell," Penny said miserably. "It must have happened early this morning."

"Call the Garda." Nora's lips trembled. "Please. I can't."

Nora had known Caroline for many years, so her reaction was entirely understandable. Penny fumbled for her phone. With the tide coming in, time was of the essence. Avoiding looking at Caroline, she squinted at the ledge. It was higher than the surrounding ground, so hopefully it would stay dry longer.

While Nora held vigil, Penny called the Garda, getting the same dispatcher as when they'd reported Kenneth's accident. "It's Penny Cavanagh. There's been a terrible accident." *Another one.* Her voice trembled, and she had to take a few deep breaths before she could continue. "We're out at Gleason's Caravan Park, on the shore below the headland. Someone has fallen off the cliff—" She swallowed hard. "And she's dead. Caroline Pierce is her name."

"Did you see her fall?" the dispatcher asked.

"No," Penny said. "She's been missing all morning, and we were searching for her."

"Stay put. Someone will be there soon. Don't touch anything."

"We won't." Penny stared at the waves moving closer every minute. "You might have to send a boat. The tide is coming in."

"Go back to the beach and wait there," the dispatcher said.

"We don't need to do a water rescue today as well."

"I'll take some pictures of the cliff," Penny offered. "So they can find her location easily."

"Only the cliff," the dispatcher warned. "And no social media. The detective inspector would not be pleased."

"Got it," Penny said. The dispatcher disconnected, and Penny took several shots of the cliff face above where Caroline lay. She made sure to get the contour of the land above so the rescuers could easily find the exact spot.

"What are you doing?" Nora asked. "Detective work?"

"Not exactly." Penny explained her photography. Then she caught sight of something glinting on a small ledge part of the way down the cliff. "What's that?"

She zoomed in and took a picture. When she enlarged the image even more, she realized it was a key chain made of gold-tinted metal. She should mention it to the Garda in case it was important, even though any visitor to the caravan park might have dropped it.

"The dispatcher said we should wait on the beach," Penny said. "I told her about the tide coming in."

Nora threw a worried frown in Caroline's direction. "It's a difficult spot. I hope they can reach her."

"Me too." Penny put her phone away and began moving along the shore. "Coming?"

Corky was happy to return to the beach, where he ran to and fro, barking at the waves and nosing into the seaweed and other debris on the sand. Penny and Nora found rocks to sit on.

"I'd better call Oliver," Nora said. "Better for him to hear it from me than the Garda." Her movements were slow as she took out her phone.

Penny didn't blame her cousin for being reluctant to make the call. Even if Oliver and Caroline were divorced, it would be a huge blow.

Nora started to touch the screen then paused. "Penny, when do you think Caroline fell?"

Penny shrugged. "Hard to say." The Garda would probably be able to figure it out, but that wasn't something she cared to ponder. "Early this morning, before anyone got up?"

"What if it was last night?" Nora's voice was tense. "I saw Oliver walking outside the caravans a little after midnight."

"What were you doing up at midnight?" Penny had been fast asleep by then.

"I had some ideas for future paintings, so I sketched them out. You know how it is."

The implication of Nora's words hit Penny. "Are you thinking that *Oliver* pushed her? No way, Nora. It was an accident."

"Was it?" Nora asked. "Maybe I shouldn't tell him. Or the others. Let the Garda spring it on everyone."

Penny's heart sank. Had someone from the dig team killed Caroline? Or maybe it had been an accident, a scuffle at the top of the cliff resulting in a tragic fall. Had she and Nora really ended up in the middle of yet another murder? "Unbelievable," she murmured.

"No kidding," Nora agreed. Although she still held the phone, she didn't make the call.

Noticing movement on the bluff path, Penny recognized Oliver on his way down. "Here comes Oliver anyway. We're going to have to tell him."

Oliver acted normal, waving and smiling when he spotted them sitting on the rocks. "I take it you didn't find her?" he asked when he was within earshot.

"Oliver," Nora said. "You need to sit down." She gestured toward a nearby rock.

"Why?" Oliver frowned as he lowered himself to the hard surface.

"Did you talk to Caroline? Is she still mad at me?"

"Why would she be mad at you?" Penny asked.

Oliver shifted on the rock, not meeting her gaze. "We had a few words last night. I don't agree with some of her decisions about the dig."

Was that all? Penny wished she didn't have to ask the question, even if only in her mind.

"We did see Caroline," Nora said slowly.

"Why didn't you say so?" Oliver leaped up from the rock. "Where is she?" He was poised as if to run and find her.

"She had an accident." Nora's tone was dull and colorless. "Oliver, she's dead."

"What?" His shout was swallowed by the wind and the waves crashing on the shore. "Where is she?"

Penny got up and grabbed his jacket sleeve. "Oliver, please. The Garda are on their way. You need to wait for them."

"The Garda?" Oliver's complexion paled, and he sat rather hastily on the rock again. "She really is dead, then."

"We weren't joking," Nora said sharply. "I also saw you out last night, so if you have anything to tell the Garda, you had better."

His chin jutted out. "Like what? You surely don't think that I—"

Nora stared toward the encroaching tide. "I don't think anything right now. It's all too awful."

Resting his elbow on his knee, Oliver put a hand to his mouth. Penny thought she saw the glitter of tears in his eyes. Corky leaned against him, trying to provide comfort.

"I'm so sorry," Penny said. "I know she meant a lot to you."

His laugh was cracked. "At one time, she was my whole world. Until that blew up in my face."

Penny thought about Caroline's challenging personality. Oliver's troubled relationship with her was to be expected, since they were once married. Barry Danvers didn't like her, or at least he opposed her plans for the Lady. What about Lee and Paige? Did either of them hold a grudge against Caroline as well?

Noticing the direction of her thoughts, Penny shook her head. She was already lining up suspects and trying to discern motives when there was no real evidence that Caroline had met with anything more than an accident. She was really getting ahead of herself—and the Garda.

Soon, they saw two officers making their way down the bluff path. Corky ran to meet them. Penny recognized Babcock and Chambley.

"So we meet again," Chambley said drily, receiving a glare from his superior.

After a minimal greeting, Detective Inspector Babcock got to the point. "Tell us what happened."

Penny and Nora took them through the sequence of events, with Oliver throwing in an occasional comment.

"You're Oliver Turnbull, correct?" Babcock asked. "You came to the hit-and-run scene."

"I did," Oliver said. "Caroline replaced Kenneth, who is still in the hospital."

Both gardaí appeared taken aback. "Let me get this straight," Babcock said. "Both leaders of this expedition have met with accidents?"

"Within days of each other," Chambley added.

Babcock continued to stare at Oliver. "I'd like to interview you in depth later. Right now, we need to retrieve Ms. Pierce before the tide comes in. Come with me, Chambley." She pointed at the trio. "You can go up to the camp and wait."

"I have pictures of the cliff where she is," Penny said. "I thought they might be helpful in finding her."

Babcock pulled out her phone. "Send them to me."

After Penny did that, the gardaí started making their way along the shore, pausing for Babcock to speak into her radio. An official-looking boat appeared out on the water, making its way toward the island.

Oliver squared his shoulders. "Well, I suppose we should go." He began trudging through the sand to the path.

Nora grabbed Corky's leash, and they followed Oliver.

"Cup of tea?" Penny offered when they reached the caravan park. Making tea would give her something to do and provide warm comfort to the grievers.

"That'd be nice," Nora said.

Lee and Paige were already in the dining area, notebooks open and chatting. "Where have you been?" Lee asked.

"What are the Garda doing here?" Paige asked, her tone sharp. "They wouldn't tell me a thing."

Oliver pulled out a chair. "I have bad news." He swallowed. "Caroline is dead."

Both archaeologists jumped up, Lee giving a bellow while Paige shrieked, "What? How?"

"She fell." Penny pointed to the bluff. "Right there." She went over to the stove to check the kettle for water. It was full, so she switched on the gas.

"No," Lee said. "I don't believe it. Caroline isn't that stupid."

Nora put up a hand. "We've given you the news, but that's it. The Garda probably don't want us discussing it."

"Why?" Paige asked. "They don't think one of us pushed her, do they?"

"I have no idea what they think," Nora said. "But I'd prefer not to get on their bad side, okay?"

"I'm sure they'll give us an update when they return," Oliver said.

Other Garda vehicles were now pulling in. Officers climbed out, some with ropes and other gear. Penny guessed that they were still debating how to get to Caroline safely, either from above or by water.

Her belly clenched with dread. *Poor Caroline.* She pulled out cups, tea bags, milk, and sugar, making sure there were enough for the Garda as well. Nora found a tin of assorted biscuits and put it on the table.

Penny poured cups of tea and handed them around. Apparently taking Nora's warning seriously, no one said anything while the Garda worked.

A pickup rattled up the lane. After pulling to a squeaking stop, Carroll Gleason got out and trotted to the dining area.

"What's all this?" Carroll asked, waving at the gardaí. "I had to hear about it from someone at the store." He rested his hands on his hips. "If anything happens on my property, I want to be told about it."

Oliver rose to his feet. "I'm sorry, Carroll. The Garda got here moments ago. There's been a terrible accident." His mouth opened and shut a few times, but no sound came out. He seemed unable to voice the news.

"Caroline Pierce, the dig's new leader, fell off the cliff," Nora said. "It's a terrible tragedy, so please give us a break."

Carroll took a step back, staring at the cliff top where the Garda worked. "Sorry for your loss," he mumbled. Then his face set into a sneer. "I suppose you're going to sue us now because some woman got too close to the edge?"

"I hadn't thought about it," Oliver said coldly. "Until you mentioned it, anyway."

The other man made a disgusted sound before stalking away toward the Garda.

"They really should put up a fence," Lee put in.

"I'm sure they will now," Paige said. "Always after the horse bolts, right?"

Oliver took a few sips of tea, a brooding expression on his face. "We're not going out to the island today. After the Garda are finished here, I still want to visit Kenneth. The poor chap is languishing alone in the hospital."

Penny had forgotten about their plan. "I'd still like to go," she said, thinking maybe he was in good enough shape that she could ask a question or two. Had he seen who hit him? Or anything at all?

Had Caroline seen who pushed her—if she had been pushed?

She thought of the key chain on the cliff. Maybe it was a clue. She brought up the picture again, but she couldn't pick out any new details. Checking her messages, she noticed that she hadn't sent the photo to Babcock along with the cliff photos. She texted the image with a note saying the item might be a clue and apologizing for not sharing it earlier.

She didn't expect an answer and was surprised when a thumbs-up emoji came right back. At least she was helping a little. That made her feel useful.

A young female garda came over to the table. "Which one of you is Penny Cavanagh?"

Penny raised her hand. "I am."

"Come with me. We're doing preliminary interviews over there." The garda pointed at a picnic table a distance away.

The officer wanted the barest facts of what Penny had seen and done, so she was finished quickly.

Nora went next. When she returned, face stony, she said, "Let's get out of here for a while, Penny."

Oliver said he would visit Kenneth after his own interview, so they set off for the hospital without him. Nora considered leaving Corky in the caravan but was worried he would bark, and the others were likely too distracted to keep an eye on him. They took him along, planning to park in the shade and keep the visit short.

"Did you tell them about seeing Oliver last night?" Penny asked.

Nora winced. "I had to, but what a thing to do to a friend. Point the Garda at him, I mean."

Penny could sympathize with her cousin's dilemma. "I'm sure he'll understand. The main thing is finding out what happened to Caroline."

"You're right. Maybe he saw or heard something important. I can't imagine him pushing her off a cliff."

As they crossed the causeway to the mainland, Penny found herself able to draw her first full breath since they'd found Caroline. She rolled down the window and inhaled the salty air, letting the wind sweep through her hair.

The hospital was a small, neat building a short distance off the main road, easily found via a multitude of signs. There weren't many cars in the visitor lot, and Nora found a shady spot under a thick, leafy tree.

Before they went in, Nora filled Corky's water dish and gave him a couple of treats to tide him over. "We'll be back soon," she told him. "We'll have a good romp later, I promise."

He watched, chin resting on the open window ledge as they walked away.

"Those puppy-dog eyes," Penny said.

Nora shook her head. "Tell me about it. He's a charmer."

As the double doors whooshed open to let them in, Penny saw a small gift shop in the corner of the lobby. "We should take Kenneth flowers," she suggested.

Nora changed course. "Good idea. I hate to arrive empty-handed."

With a small yet pretty arrangement in hand, they inquired at the desk for Kenneth's room number, then took the elevator to the third floor.

Kenneth's room door stood ajar. He was watching soccer on television, left leg in traction, his right arm in a cast, and a bandage around his head.

Nora knocked on the doorjamb. "Hello," she said, then identified herself and Penny. "Are you up for visitors?"

His eyes lit up, and he turned down the volume. "You're from the dig. Please do come in. It's not fancy, but it's all mine for the moment." He chuckled.

He had remembered their names and was in good spirits, both good signs.

Penny placed the flowers on the wide windowsill, then she and Nora both found chairs.

"How are things at the dig?" Kenneth asked. "I understand Caroline came on board. She likes projects in west Ireland. Her old stomping grounds, you know."

With a shared glance, Nora and Penny decided not to mention Caroline's death. It might upset Kenneth and cause a setback in his healing.

"I didn't realize Caroline was from Ireland," Nora said.

"She's not," Kenneth corrected. "She's from London, born and bred. Her mother's family came from around here, though."

Penny filed away the interesting fact. "Kenneth, I'm not sure if you remember, but Nora and I came across you after your accident. We were on our way to the caravan park."

A confused expression drifted across his face. "I don't remember that. Don't remember much until I woke up here. The doctor said I probably won't. Did you call the ambulance?"

"We did," Penny said, then gently added, "Do you remember anything before the accident?"

"A garda asked me about that too." Kenneth frowned in concentration. "No, nothing new. I heard a vehicle approaching and saw a flash of red out of the corner of my eye. Then, bam! Out like a light."

For the rest of the visit with Kenneth, Penny pondered what he'd said. A red vehicle. No one who worked on the dig had a red car. Carroll's truck was black.

"We'll get out of your hair," Nora said after a little while. "You need your rest."

"My beauty sleep, you mean," Kenneth said. "Though no amount of sleep will help this mug." He chuckled. "Thank you for stopping by. And for calling the ambulance."

"Our pleasure," Penny told him.

"I wouldn't mind updates on the dig now and then," he added wistfully. "It is such an exciting project."

Penny almost blurted out the news about the gold coin, but Nora put a quieting hand on her arm. "We'll let Oliver give you the official reports," Nora told Kenneth. "I'll tell him what you said."

"I appreciate that." Kenneth's expression became thoughtful. "Oliver is a good lad. Not sure why they didn't promote him. He's certainly earned it."

"We were wondering that ourselves," Penny put in. "Then we met Caroline."

"Yes, she's something else all right," Kenneth said. "I wouldn't be surprised if she weaseled her way into that assignment over him through some underhanded means. If you get in her way—well, she is perfectly capable of making your life miserable. Many have discovered that to their regret."

Penny felt an icy shiver at his assessment of Caroline's character. Had her antagonistic behavior finally caught up to her, resulting in her murder?

8

On the way back to the caravan park, Nora said, "I had no idea Caroline had relatives here. They weren't at her wedding."

"I wonder if Oliver knows," Penny said. "He never mentioned it, did he?"

"No. Maybe they're all gone."

To Penny's relief, the Garda were no longer at the caravan park, leaving behind nothing but a strip of caution tape across the door of the caravan that had belonged to Kenneth, then Caroline. Her pulse began to pound. Had the Garda come up with an explanation for her fall? Maybe it had been a simple accident, and all of Penny's musings about murder had been baseless.

"I'm going to go find Oliver," Nora said when they climbed out of the car. "Coming?"

"You bet." Penny let Corky out of the back. He ran around in circles, chasing scent trails with his nose. "He's going to be busy for a while." With all the people passing through the park on their way back and forth to the cliff, there must be all kinds of enticing aromas.

A glance at the dining area revealed that Oliver wasn't there, so they went to his caravan next. They were rapping on the door when Paige stepped out of her own trailer. "He's down at the Garda station."

"What?" Nora took a step backward and down, almost landing on Penny's sneaker. "Did they arrest him?"

"Not sure," Paige answered. "I saw him get into the car—that's all."

Without another word, she went back inside, the door shutting firmly behind her.

Penny wanted to go over and demand answers, but that probably wouldn't help matters. "I wonder if Lee knows anything."

Nora checked the parking area. "His car is missing. We'll have to wait."

"Tea?" Penny offered, not having much else to give.

"Sure." Nora stomped across the grass. "Why not?"

They had just settled down with mugs when a Garda vehicle pulled down the lane. An officer climbed out and opened the back door, and Oliver emerged.

Nora jumped to her feet. "Thank goodness." Setting down her mug, she took off across the grass, Corky yapping in excitement right behind her.

Penny followed at a more sedate pace, although she was glad to see Oliver's return and eager to get an update.

"You're free." Nora threw her arms around Oliver. "We were so worried."

He squeezed her back. "So was I. They had me pinned under lights, questions hitting me from all directions—"

"Seriously?" Nora rested her hands on her hips.

"No. I'm joking. It wasn't fun, though." He ran a finger around the collar of his polo. "I'm parched."

"The kettle is hot," Penny said.

On the way back to the dining area, Oliver detoured to tear the caution tape off Caroline's door. "They said they were done in here."

Penny was glad to hear that, because the mobile home held a lot of vital information for the dig. Did the trailer also contain clues the Garda had overlooked? Penny thought maybe they should take a peek after getting an update from Oliver.

They didn't speak until they were all seated with their tea. "The Garda believe Caroline was pushed," Oliver said baldly. "And right now, I'm their top suspect. I'm her ex-husband, and she was hired over my head on my current project. I have to confess that even to me that sounds pretty bad."

"I'm so sorry, Oliver," Nora said. "Please forgive me."

He tilted his head. "For what?"

Nora wouldn't meet his gaze. "I told them you were out and about late the night she died. That's a huge reason that they suspect you, isn't it?"

"Probably," Oliver said. "Besides the fact I'm her ex-husband and professional rival. Little details like that." He put a hand on Nora's forearm. "Don't fret, Nora. You had to tell them. Put it this way—you saved me from the temptation of trying to lie and making things worse for myself."

Nora glanced up, a small smile on her face. "That's a relief. So, what were you talking to Caroline about?"

Oliver made a face. "The dig. We were butting heads over how to handle the coin discovery. I wanted to hold off making a big deal until we found more. She wanted to call our department head today and start ramping up the publicity machine."

"What would be the advantage of that?" Penny asked. "As soon as any word leaks out, you'll be overrun by lookie-loos."

"Exactly," Oliver said. "With zero security budget as it stands. Caroline's rationale was that it would boost the dig's profile and we could ask for more funding on the speculation that there is treasure. I preferred not to go that route."

"Did you come to any resolution?" Nora asked.

"Sort of," Oliver said. "She agreed to give it another week or until we found another coin, whichever came first. Then we said good night and I went in, leaving her quite alive."

"Besides her argument with you, how did she seem?" Penny asked. Oliver thought for a moment. "Something was bothering her. Not sure what, though. She wouldn't have told me if I asked. She was quite secretive, which was one of many problems in our marriage."

Penny saw an opening for another of her questions. "Were you aware that Caroline's mother came from this area?"

Oliver sat back. "No, I was not. Who told you that?"

"Kenneth," Nora said. "We didn't tell him about Caroline. We were afraid he'd have a setback. He knew that Caroline had taken his place, so we spoke about her briefly."

Pressing his lips together, Oliver shook his head. "Like I said, she was secretive. Her mother died before we met, so we never did talk much about that side of the family. You'd think us coming here to work would bring up the topic, though."

"You'd think," Penny agreed.

"How is Kenneth?" Oliver asked, changing the subject. "I feel remiss not going to see him."

"You were rather busy," Nora said, getting up. "I want another cup. Anyone else?"

"Yes, please." Penny handed Nora her mug, then returned her attention to Oliver. "Kenneth was in good spirits. He gave us a clue as well. He caught a glimpse of red right before he was hit. I think that means it was a red vehicle."

"Red, huh?" Oliver's gaze went reflexively to the parking lot. None of the dig team drove a red car, not even Lee, who was still gone. "I hope they find the driver. If it was a tourist, though, they probably never will."

Penny imagined a visitor hitting Kenneth by accident and then driving away without reporting it, eager to put the island and the incident behind them. "That would be awful."

Oliver sighed. "Well, I might as well try to get some work done. That never fails me."

"Seriously, Oliver?" Nora frowned. "I thought maybe you'd take at least one day off."

Her friend shrugged. "I can't. Or maybe the truth is that I won't. Sitting around and brooding won't help anything. We can't stop the dig either. Not with funders and the university having invested so much. We have to reach certain milestones this summer or we'll be closed down for good."

Penny sympathized with his predicament. "Plus, there's the coin to consider. You need to figure out if there are more while you have the chance."

"You're right, Penny. If there is a sizable hoard, we need to find and secure it even if it has been hidden for millennia. Once word gets out, there will be no stopping the response." Picking up his mug, Oliver pushed back his chair and stood. "I need to go have a very difficult conversation with the department head. See you later."

At loose ends for the moment, Penny focused on meal planning, thinking light and simple would be good for dinner. People probably didn't have much appetite. She certainly did not.

"What do you think of a salad bar for dinner?" she asked Nora. "I can put out cold meats and cheese for toppings."

"Sounds fine," Nora said. "No one will want to eat much anyway." She finished her tea and got up. "I'm going to take Corky for a walk."

Penny took a variety of vegetables out of the refrigerator and started chopping and dicing, appreciating the soothing nature of the task. Although she had barely met Caroline, she was deeply disturbed and unsettled. Had one of the team pushed Caroline? Or had it been a late-night visitor to the park?

She must have been sleeping soundly because she hadn't heard a thing. No arguments or screams in the night. If someone hadn't wanted their vehicle to be heard, they could have parked along the road and walked down the lane.

The fact that Caroline might have a connection to Anoach Island intrigued Penny. It was the outlier, the fact that didn't fit. Otherwise, the solution would seem simple. An angry ex-husband frustrated at her reappearance in his life—and suddenly in charge of his pet project.

Penny's cell phone rang. She glanced at the screen. *Finn.* She answered and put it on speakerphone. "Hello. How are you?"

"A better question would be, how are you?" Finn sounded concerned. "Just heard the news of an untimely death on Anoach Island. And how my girlfriend discovered the body."

Penny's shoulders slumped. "I'm sorry, Finn. I should have called you sooner. I figured you were busy."

His voice softened. "I was, actually. At a training facility and out of reach."

"Hold on." Penny put her knife down and sat, then took the phone off speaker. "It was awful, Finn. So awful." She explained how Caroline had been missing, thought to have gone for a walk. Then her and Nora's ill-fated search, resulting in the terrible discovery. "No one's been arrested," she concluded. "Yet. According to Oliver, he's the top suspect."

"Her ex-husband? That's to be expected." Finn was silent for a moment. "Give me the rundown of the other people staying there."

Penny gaped at her phone. Then she whispered, "Are you investigating?"

"Not officially," came his quick answer. "There might be one or two things I can do from here, though. If you weren't involved, I wouldn't dream of it. You might say I have a vested interest in making sure they're thorough."

Until he said that, Penny hadn't realized quite how much she had come to count on Finn. He was like a rock-solid wall at her back.

"I was chopping vegetables for salad," she told Finn. "Give me a second to clean up, then I'll go to our caravan to talk." She didn't want to have their discussion in the open air where anyone might overhear her.

A few minutes later, she was curled up on her bed, the windows and her bedroom door shut. She told him about the other members of the party, Kenneth's remark that Caroline was a very difficult person, and Barry Danvers's anger about Caroline's interest in the Lady of the Bog. Penny also passed on that Caroline's mother had come from the area, hoping that Finn could trace that lineage. The Garda had ready access to vital statistics databases such as birth certificates, marriage licenses, and deaths. Penny could search them as well, but it would take a lot longer and be more hit-or-miss since she didn't have Caroline's complete information.

"I'm so glad you're helping," Penny said. "It's a huge weight off my mind."

Finn harrumphed into the phone. "I wish I could be there. Unfortunately, I'm stuck here for a few days longer. If I leave early, I'll forfeit all the time I've already put in and have to take the course again."

"Don't do that. I'm fine. Really. Hopefully the case will break in the next couple of days, and we can all relax."

"I hope so too. I'm going to pull a few strings and get an update. If you learn anything that might remotely have bearing on Caroline's death, please call me. Send a text. A note by seagull. Whatever."

Penny laughed. "That's a cute idea. Carrier gull." She pictured one flapping away with a tiny canister strapped to its leg.

They chatted for a few more minutes before reluctantly hanging up. Penny missed Finn, missed their daily time together. Phone calls were no substitute.

She was still moping on her bed when Nora stuck her head in. "Oliver is in Caroline's caravan sorting through papers. Want to go over?"

That caught her interest. Penny scrambled off the bed. "Absolutely I do."

Could they find a clue to Caroline's death?

"Dig central," Penny said when they stepped into the adjacent trailer. In contrast to their caravan, Kenneth's former lair was set up like an office with a desk, shelving, and work tables in the sitting room area.

"Exactly." Oliver was behind the desk, leafing through files and papers. "Caroline brought a ton of her own work too. I'm trying to get it all organized."

Penny scanned the titles in one stack of books. "These are all on bog bodies. Was Caroline studying them?"

"In relation to the Lady," Oliver said. "As far as I know." He picked up an envelope. "Remember the scene with Barry? He also dropped off an official letter warning her that the Lady isn't available for testing."

Nora took the envelope, extracted the letter, and scanned the text. "He's really dead set against it. Seems a little strange."

"Agreed." Oliver continued to sort, stacking several folders to one side. "Caroline even brought college correspondence with her. These all have to do with students or faculty she supervises."

Penny didn't want to invade the privacy of the folders, but she couldn't help but notice a familiar name on one label. *Paige Matthews*. "Our Paige?" she asked.

Oliver nodded. "She's probably going for an opening we have. It's a step up."

Penny wondered if Caroline had been supportive of Paige's promotion.

Nora passed her Barry's letter. She skimmed it and gasped. "He said he's already contacted her superiors about her threats to go to his board. The conflict was really escalating."

"You'd think Barry would have ended at the bottom of the cliff," Oliver said. "Knowing Caroline, she wasn't going to take that lying down. She believed in fighting fire with fire."

Had Barry and Caroline argued on the cliff? Perhaps they'd struggled and Caroline had gone over. Barry was taller and heavier than Caroline, although the woman had been in good shape. She'd wielded a trowel for hours without complaint on the island.

Someone rapped on the door. "Penny, you're closest," Oliver said. "Do you mind?"

"Not at all." Penny pulled the handle and peered out cautiously.

Kinzi Eagan, dressed in jeans and a sweatshirt, stood at the bottom of the steps, arms folded and scowling.

Penny opened the door a little wider. "Can I help you?" she asked. She had a feeling Kinzi hadn't come to extend condolences for Caroline's death.

Kinzi hopped up the steps. "I want to speak to whoever is in charge."

"Oliver, someone is here to see you." Penny fully opened the door so Oliver could view the visitor.

He ran a hand through his hair and then stood. "Ms. Eagan. How may I help you?"

Kinzi took that as an invitation and pushed past Penny, leaving a trail of fragrant herbal scent in her wake. "The line of succession has come down to you?" she demanded of him.

"That's one way of putting it, I suppose," Oliver said. He glanced around. "I'm sorry I can't offer you a seat." All the chairs were heaped with books, papers, banker boxes, or other academic paraphernalia.

"I don't need one. Won't stay long." After seeming to settle her thoughts, Kinzi said, "I understand you want to tamper with the Lady. Take her away to be examined."

Oliver put up a hand. "Hold on. I don't want to do that. That was Caroline's project."

Kinzi opened her mouth to respond.

"Let me finish," Oliver said. "She meant to remove one hair for a very specific test. Not the whole body. There's no need to do that for those tests."

Kinzi didn't appear convinced. "No X-rays or MRIs? How about samples of bone and tissue? I've been doing my research too."

"I'm sure you have, Ms. Eagan." Oliver kept his tone even and patient. "I can assure you that I have no plans to disturb the Lady. I'm quite busy with other matters."

Kinzi scowled at him, her brow furrowing. "I don't trust you. Everyone lies."

Oliver sighed again. "I don't know what to say to convince you—"

Paige appeared in the doorway. "What's going on in here?"

The older woman whirled around, her jewelry jingling. "They're going to take the Lady away."

"Oliver?" Paige's tone was questioning.

"That isn't true," Oliver said. "It was Caroline who wanted to do more tests, and she didn't plan to remove the body to do them. But the tests are not our assignment here, so I have no intention to follow through on that at all."

To Penny's surprise, Paige came and put her arm around the troubled woman. "Would you like a cup of tea? I was about to put on the kettle in my caravan."

"Do you have builder's tea?" Kinzi asked. "I like that."

"I know you do," Paige said soothingly, guiding her out of the caravan. "Nice and strong, with a splash of milk."

Once they were gone, Nora asked, "Does Kinzi pop by often?"

"She's been haunting us ever since we got here," Oliver said. "Thankfully, Paige has taken a liking to the old bird."

"Kinzi and Barry appear to be convinced that your expedition is going to hurt the Lady somehow," Penny said. "I don't get it."

Oliver plopped back into the chair, sending it rocking. "Me neither. I'm interested in Iron Age settlements, not bog bodies. Believe me—we have plenty to keep us busy without adding a battle over a body with a whole island, and we're shorthanded. Tomorrow, it's back to the dig."

In anticipation of a full day on the small island, Penny packed a large lunch and plenty of drinks and snacks in the coolers the next morning. Oliver was eager to make up for lost time. Penny also suspected that he was eager to bury his grief and troubles in work, something the rest of the team understood.

When Carroll transported them out, a smaller skiff was tied behind his boat. "In case someone needs to go back," Oliver explained. "We really should have a boat with us at all times."

Penny agreed. Otherwise, they were stranded until a phone call reached someone on the mainland and they could make the journey out.

Carroll left them on the shore, the skiff pulled onto the rocky beach out of reach of the waves, and zoomed away. Once again, they loaded up, and with the usual complaints from Lee, carted the supplies up over the rise. Corky ran back and forth, tail wagging, as if encouraging them on.

"Cheer up," Paige told Lee. "We could find another coin today. Tell me about another job where you might discover treasure."

Lee cracked a grin. "Good point." He began to move faster. "I'll do this all day if it means we find a hoard."

"What's the plan, Oliver?" Paige asked. "Dig in my trench? That makes sense to me."

"Agreed," Oliver said. "We'll have two diggers and two sifters today. Nora, you can continue sketching. We still need to record everything."

"Can't throw protocol to the wind over treasure," Lee said.

To Penny's relief, the site appeared undisturbed. In the back of her mind, she'd imagined the news of the coin leaking out somehow and bringing treasure hunters to Beag Anoach. Caroline hadn't had a chance to tell anyone at the university, as far as she knew. The coin was still top secret.

After organizing the coolers under the tarp for the eating area, Penny went over to the trench. There was already a heap of soil for her to sift, and she readily got to work. A few more fragments from the past showed up as she went, including pottery shards and an iron spearhead.

"Now that is a nice find," Oliver said, studying the object. "You can see the caliber of workmanship in the finely honed curves."

Penny was struck by how completely the former settlement had vanished, leaving a few bare clues to a former way of life. She was glad she'd seen the displays at the museum. Otherwise her imagination would have failed her. A thousand years ago, the very bluff she stood on had teemed with life and laughter and activity. That day, however, the sea wind blew incessantly over the rolling ground, and the lone sounds were an occasional bird cry and the chink and scrape of the tools.

"Peaceful out here, isn't it?" Paige said, using the back of her hand to wipe her dusty face. "There's nowhere I'd rather be."

Lee made an amused sound. "You mean you prefer it to the politics and problems of university life? But it's such a treat dealing with red tape and complaining students."

Oliver gave a grunt of agreement. "Tell me about it."

"All a means to an end," Paige said. "Without the university, I wouldn't get to come out here."

Even after being on the dig for such a short time, Penny could tell it wasn't a fast track to glory. Reputations and bodies of work in archaeology were literally built inch by inch. It wasn't a profession for an impatient person, that was for sure.

Penny was about to suggest a tea break when Carroll's boat came roaring back toward the island.

"I wonder what he wants." Oliver climbed out of the trench and stretched, watching.

Dread gripped Penny. Had something else happened? Or had the Garda sent Carroll to fetch someone? Maybe they were ready to make an arrest. But surely the Garda would come themselves in that event.

Lee squinted into the distance, hand shading his eyes. "Looks like Barry is with him."

Paige pushed her trowel into the sand. "Him again? I wonder what bee is in his bonnet today." Her remark drew a few laughs.

"Three guesses," Lee said. In unison, he and Paige intoned, "The Lady." More laughter.

"I'll put on the kettle," Penny said. They had a small gas camping stove as part of the setup, and she preferred fresh boiled water to stale from the thermoses. She blamed it on the influence of the tearoom's sommelier, Ian Duffy.

The others joined her under the canopy, silent as they watched Barry and Carroll come over the rise and down into the camp. When Barry spotted them, he broke into a trot.

"I know you lot did it!" he shouted after huffing and puffing to a stop. He waved a fist. "You stole the Lady."

9

A dumbfounded silence met Barry's claim.

Finally, Oliver spoke. "What on earth are you talking about, Danvers?"

The sincere confusion in his tone silenced Barry for an instant. His mouth flapped a couple of times and then he blurted, "The Lady. She's gone. From the museum."

Penny imagined the empty case with horror. Who would do such a thing? And why? Surely the other artifacts would be more attractive to a thief since they would be easier to transport and sell.

"That's not good," Lee said. "Doesn't she need a controlled environment?"

Barry seemed to rally. "Exactly. Whoever did this is criminal. And I intend to prosecute."

"Don't you have a security system?" Paige asked. "Sensors? Cameras?"

Barry dug his toe into the grass. "We couldn't afford sensors." He swallowed. "The cameras haven't been working well for a while." As he glanced around the circle, his bravado dissolved even further.

Lee wasn't going to let him off the hook. "Let me get this straight. You allowed security to lapse at your museum and now you're surprised someone took advantage? Rather than flinging accusations around, maybe you should remedy the issue. As I recall, you have some pretty nice artifacts in there. You don't want them to disappear too, do you?"

Barry's chin quivered. "You're right. I was so shocked when I saw she was gone that I didn't even think about that." He blinked rapidly.

"She's the centerpiece of the museum, an icon in our village. What will we be without her?"

Considering that the Lady was the main attraction on Anoach Island, Penny saw his point.

"I'm sorry, Barry," Oliver said. "I hope you find her soon. I can assure you that none of us had anything to do with it."

Penny scanned the circle, hoping Oliver was right. The theft of the Lady was another twist in a very unsettling series of events—Kenneth's hit-and-run, the break-in at his caravan, and Caroline's death.

Carroll had wandered off and climbed down into the other trench.

"Hey," Paige cried as she ran toward him. "What are you doing?"

"Looking around," Carroll said, a whine in his voice. "Why shouldn't I?"

"Because we record every layer, in order," Paige said. "You're messing up our work."

"Doesn't look like much to me," Carroll said, lingering. "You find any gold yet?"

A start of surprise rippled through the team. Penny hoped it hadn't been too obvious to Barry and Carroll.

"We're searching for artifacts from an Iron Age village," Paige answered, skirting the question. "That is our main purpose."

Carroll cocked an eyebrow at her as he clambered out. "I heard there was a hoard here somewhere. Been a rumor all my life."

"We aren't here for rumors," Paige said. "We base our work on facts."

"Okay." Carroll's smile was impertinent. "I'll leave you to your *work*."

No one said anything as Barry and Carroll trudged away. Once they were over the rise, Penny asked, "Who wants tea?" She found a tin of biscuits and plated them while Lee opened folding chairs. Nora decided against tea and carried her sketch pad to a boulder several yards away, Corky sprawled at her feet.

They soon heard the roar of Carroll's boat engine.

"If Carroll knew about the hoard, others must," Paige said.

"A good reason to camp out here," Oliver said. "We need to guard the site."

"Let's hope it doesn't rain." Paige shrugged. "Although that would probably discourage treasure hunters."

"Maybe the one coin was it," Lee said. When they all stared at him, he shrugged. "It's possible."

Penny certainly hoped not. What fun was that? Changing the subject, she said, "I hope Barry finds the Lady soon. She was a pretty rare find too, wasn't she?"

Lee snorted. "I'll say. Very few intact bog bodies have been discovered throughout Europe. Most of them have been found in Scandinavia."

"The key is undisturbed bogs," Oliver said. "Who knows how many bones are buried down there? They sink into the mire and are never seen again."

Paige sat with her phone, flicking through with a grimace. "The service is awful out here."

"That's to be expected," Lee said. "When this village was here, messages were carried on horseback or on foot. Talk about slow mail."

"I couldn't bear it," Paige said. "I'm too much of a modern girl."

"Says the archaeologist," Lee remarked.

"The past is fascinating and crucial to study, yes." Paige pulled a face. "But I wouldn't want to live there."

Penny checked her phone, relieved to find that she had two bars, even if they flickered. She found it amazing that cell service had become available in many remote places thanks to towers and satellites.

Oliver had been jotting notes in a spiral-bound book. "What do you think of camping out here, team? The weather is supposed to be okay for the next few days. We really need to get caught up."

"Why not?" Lee shrugged. "We brought tents, right? Penny, you'll need to pack plenty of provisions for us."

"I can do that," Penny agreed. It would mean cooking on the small stove, which would be a challenge, but she didn't mind. She'd make a one-pot meal for dinner and a big fry-up for breakfast.

"How about tomorrow night, then?" Oliver suggested. "When we get back this afternoon, we'll pack. For now, let's get back to work."

Penny went over to Nora to share the plan. "We're going to camp out here tomorrow night. So we can get more done."

"That sounds like an adventure," Nora said. "I'm glad we brought our sleeping bags."

Penny thought the plan sounded exciting as well. Then she thought of the blinking phone service bars. She shivered. Hopefully nothing else would happen while they were staying on the island. Options for escaping or calling for help might be limited.

They worked until around two in the afternoon, when they broke for lunch. So far, they hadn't found another coin, which was discouraging—to Penny, at least. The others seemed to take it in stride.

Penny served sandwiches with sides of potato salad, sliced vegetables, and chips, and after a brief break, they went back to the trenches.

"We'll go until six," Oliver said. "Take advantage of the light."

An hour later, Lee, who was working near Penny, let out a groan. "What is it?" she asked, alarmed. "Did you hurt yourself?"

Rather than showing her a cut or scratch, he held a hand to his belly. "I don't feel good."

"Oh no. Are you coming down with something?" Penny hoped not.

An illness sweeping through the team would slow them down further. He shook his head. "I think it was the potato salad." He put a fist to his mouth. "Yep. That was it."

"What's going on?" Oliver called from a distance away.

"Lee doesn't feel well." Penny swallowed, not wanting to voice the words. "He thinks he has food poisoning." She'd bought the salad already prepared. Had it gone bad and she hadn't noticed? She sure hoped not. "How does everyone else feel?"

"I'm fine," Paige called. Nora chimed in with agreement.

"It's probably me." Lee wrinkled his nose. "I have a sensitive stomach."

Oliver rested his hands on his hips, studying the other man. "Are you going to make it? Or do you want to head back?"

"Go back, I think," Lee said. "Hopefully it will work through my system fast."

Penny made a mental note to toss the rest of the potato salad. She wouldn't buy any more prepared foods from the general store.

"Take the small boat, then." Oliver pulled out his phone. "I'm going to double-check with Carroll first." After sending and receiving a series of texts, he said, "He's coming at six. So go ahead, Lee. Hope you feel better."

"Enjoy your rest," Paige called out teasingly once Lee had gathered his pack and was leaving. She laughed. "Serves you right if I find the next coin."

"I hope you do," Lee said before continuing on.

"Are you sure you all feel okay?" Penny asked. "I'm worried that I gave you spoiled food by accident."

Once again, they all reassured her. "Lee does have a finicky stomach," Paige said. "It's simply one of those things. Don't blame yourself."

Nonetheless, Penny made a mental note to go through the food inventory and double-check the freshness of everything, especially the ingredients she was bringing to the island for the overnight. She also intended to have plenty of cold packs for the coolers.

Despite losing Lee, they made good progress over the rest of the afternoon. They found several artifacts, including pottery beads, more metal tool fragments, and parts of a cauldron, a sign that the spot was once a home. No gold, though.

"At least we know where the hoard isn't," Paige said.

Penny was glad to see Carroll arrive in the boat. She couldn't wait to take a shower and get a good night's sleep. The next few nights, they'd be roughing it.

"You're up with the birds," Nora said as she wandered into the dining area, stretching and yawning. "I noticed you were already packed."

Penny paused in making her list. "I packed enough clothes for a couple of days, as well as my sleeping bag and pillows. Right now, I'm planning meals." She was thinking of canned food and packaged meals that didn't require refrigeration. Better safe than sorry when it came to food spoiling. "I wonder how Lee is doing."

"I'll go check." Nora strode off, Corky accompanying her.

Oliver was next to appear. "Good morning, Penny." He checked the kettle, which was gently steaming, and made a cup of tea.

Penny filled him in on her meal plans. "I'll need to go to the store for some items. I'll try not to hold you up too long."

"We can go ahead with Carroll, and you can take the small boat," Oliver said. "Can you operate a boat with a motor?"

"Yes," Penny said cautiously. "But it's been a while."

"I'll give you a refresher course before we take off. The boat's not fast, but it will get you to the island." Oliver squinted at the water.

"It's a calm day. You'll be fine."

Penny hoped so. The trip was testing her abilities in many more ways than she had anticipated, which she supposed was a good thing. Worst case scenario, she could always call Carroll to come take her out to the island, though she preferred to avoid that. There was something about him she didn't like.

"Give me Carroll's number in case we need him," she said anyway. "It's good to have a backup plan."

"Sure thing." Oliver read out the digits, and Penny added the contact to her phone.

Nora came trotting back. "Lee is still not back to normal," she told them.

"Really?" Oliver frowned. "I'd better go talk to him. Maybe he should see a doctor."

As he walked away, Nora said to Penny, "He didn't look that bad to me. So, whatever it is, he's getting over it."

"I'm glad to hear that." Penny still worried that he'd gotten ill from something she'd prepared. "Maybe I can bring him out later, after I buy the food." She filled Nora in on the plan.

"Good for you," Nora said. "You're getting really adventurous."

"Not by choice," Penny said with a laugh. "I don't want to hold up the team. It's probably going to take me until about noon to get out there."

"Take your time," Nora said. "We'll keep plugging away."

Penny made Nora a cup of tea. "It's really strange about the Lady, isn't it? Who would steal her?"

"Good question." Nora pulled out her phone and tapped the screen. "No sign of a bog body on the auction sites."

That startled a laugh from Penny. "You think someone would do that?"

"Probably not publicly," Nora said. "Black market, maybe. Some collectors don't mind buying stolen goods, even though they can't tell anyone."

"I wonder if Barry reported it to the Garda," Penny said. "They can put her on a watch list." On an impulse, she took out her phone and sent Finn a text. *Another crime. The bog body is missing from the museum.*

His reply came quickly. *Seriously? That's a new one on me.*

No kidding. They literally stole her from the case. Penny found and attached a picture of the exhibit.

My goodness, Penny. Never a dull moment.

Very true. We're camping on Beag Anoach tonight, just so you know. Service might be spotty. Given everything that had happened, Penny didn't want him to worry if he suddenly couldn't contact her.

Thanks for the heads-up. Any news about Caroline?

Nothing. No arrests, no new information.

Be careful.

I will.

"Finn?" Nora guessed. "How is he?"

Penny glanced at the string of messages. "Oops. I didn't even ask."

How are you?

Great. Almost done with my course. Acing it.

Hurray! Not surprised, but still proud of you.

Thanks. I miss you.

I miss you too. Can't wait to see you soon. Penny noticed she was smiling as she signed off. Finn had that effect on her.

Corky trotted over and nudged Penny's knee. She gave him a thorough patting. "Want me to bring Corky with me later? Then you won't have to worry about him while you're digging."

"Are you sure?" Nora asked. She opened a box of cereal and poured some into a bowl, then added milk.

Cereal sounded good to Penny too, so she found a bowl for herself. "Positive. He won't jump overboard or anything, will he?"

"No, he's fine in boats. Tell him to sit." Nora caught her dog's eye. "You'll listen to Aunt Penny, won't you?" His tail wagged furiously.

"He definitely understands you," Penny said. "He's such a smart boy."

After breakfast, the team loaded up for the trip to Beag Anoach. Penny promised to check in on Lee and bring him along if he was better. The small boat had enough room for two people, a dog, and provisions.

Penny puttered around cleaning up, not wanting to leave any crumbs for ants or other critters that might come along. Perishables went into the refrigerator, and she made sure all the storage boxes were locked. Food items and cookware she was taking went into crates for easy transport in the boat.

Ready to go shopping, she faced Corky, who had been watching intently the entire time. "Want to go for a ride?"

He bounded up from a lying position onto all fours, and then bounced on his paws.

Penny laughed. "Impressive reflexes. I wish I could jump up that fast."

Making sure she had her list, Penny grabbed her handbag and the dog's leash, then set off in the Peugeot.

The day was warm and sunny, and Penny drove slowly along the narrow lanes, windows open. Although she wanted to get over to the island to help, there really wasn't any hurry. She ought to slow down and smell the roses—or rather the coconut aroma of yellow gorse.

Suddenly, she realized she wasn't sure where she was. *The danger of daydreaming.* She must have taken the wrong road a couple of miles back.

Up ahead, a barn stood in an overgrown field, a narrow track leading to it. The gate was open, which gave Penny room to turn around.

As Penny backed in, cautiously checking the mirrors so she didn't hit a rock, Corky began to whine, sticking his nose out the window and sniffing enthusiastically.

"Smell something interesting, do you? All right, Corky. I'll let you out for a minute." Penny parked and switched off the engine. She climbed out, then opened the back door.

Corky took off like a rocket, directly toward the old barn.

Penny's shoulders sagged. *Apparently that's what caught his interest.* The place must still hold intriguing animal smells. "Corky," she called. "Come back." Although she tried to inject Nora's authority into her voice, she sounded rather weak.

No wonder he completely ignored her. Then, to her dismay, he went inside the barn. She'd have to go get him.

Penny grabbed the leash and set off along the lane at a trot. Why had she offered to take him? What if he kept going and got lost? Nora would never forgive her if something happened to her beloved pet.

To Penny's relief, Corky was still inside the barn when she got there. If she could get inside and leash him, they could be on their way.

The front sliding door was open a crack. "Corky?" She heard him panting in the dark somewhere.

Very little light filtered into the barn. The few lower windows were caked with dirt, and the ones above were small. As her eyes adjusted, Penny saw a newer-model red car at the very back of the barn. Apparently someone was using the barn as a garage. All the more reason to retrieve the dog and get out of there.

Then, as she tried to figure out where Corky was, something chimed in her mind. Kenneth had glimpsed something before he'd been hit. *A flash of red.*

Maybe she'd discovered why the police hadn't been able to locate the vehicle involved in the hit-and-run. It had been parked in a remote barn.

She took several cautious steps forward on the ancient, hay-strewn boards. She couldn't see the front of the car yet, so before speculating, she needed to check it over.

Corky came running up to her, tongue lolling, happy as a clam. "You're a bad boy," Penny said half-heartedly as she clipped the leash to his collar. "Don't run away like that."

His response was to lick her hand.

Holding the leash, she continued toward the car. Fortunately, there weren't many obstacles on the floor, though she saw plenty of rusty tools and other objects piled along the walls. Old stalls stood open with more stuff stacked inside them.

Who owns this barn? she wondered. As she drew closer to the car, she switched on her cell phone light and flashed it around, noticing there wasn't a license plate. Another sign that it was the mystery car.

The front of the vehicle confirmed her theory. The fender and bumper were both heavily dented, as if they'd hit something at a high speed.

She felt certain she'd unwittingly discovered the car that had hit Kenneth. But had it been an accident—or on purpose?

10

Penny winced, imagining the scene in her mind. Poor Kenneth. He was lucky to be alive.

Something creaked, and Penny jumped. Was someone in the barn? No, it was the open door swaying gently in the breeze.

She should leave before the driver came back. Taking a deep breath of dusty air, she told herself to calm down. She would take some pictures and send them to the Garda. She might be in trouble for trespassing, but she had only been following Corky. Besides, she'd solved a huge mystery.

Penny snapped a couple photos of the damage and then others of the whole car. Hopefully that would be enough to track down the owner—and convince the Garda to check out the barn too.

Although she had Detective Inspector Babcock's cell phone number, Penny called the station first, and the receptionist put Penny through to the investigator's voice mail. As she told Babcock about her discovery, however, she realized she had no idea where she was. "I'll take a picture of the barn," she said. "And check for a sign at the end of the lane."

Penny hoped Babcock wouldn't think she was a bumbling fool. To be fair, she hadn't expected to come across a vehicle suspected in a hit-and-run. She'd been chasing a naughty dog.

Before getting into the Peugeot, she took several pictures of the barn and the property in general. If the Garda were familiar with the island, they shouldn't have any trouble finding the place, even without an address. Anoach Island wasn't that large.

Once driving, Penny retraced her route to the beginning of the side road, but she didn't find a street sign. Pulling over, she sent the pictures to Babcock's cell phone with a note mentioning the lack of signage, and then continued on to the village.

As she drove past the museum, she swung into the parking lot on impulse. It bothered her that the Lady had been stolen. What a strange thing for someone to do. Had it been to prevent anyone from taking a closer look at the body and analyzing it scientifically? She wasn't sure why that would be a problem, especially if the tests wouldn't damage the Lady.

She left Corky in the car with the windows open. He appeared quite content to sprawl on the back seat after his romp at the barn.

"I'll be quick," she promised him. "One more stop at the store, and then we'll motor out to find Nora." He whined at the mention of his owner's name.

Penny noticed the lot was empty aside from the Peugeot. Had visitation already dropped due to the main attraction being gone? Or maybe it was a quiet day in general. With such nice weather, Penny was sure families wanted to be at the beach or otherwise enjoying the sunshine.

Barry frowned as she came through the door. "Back to the scene of the crime?" he sniped.

"What?" Penny stopped short so fast her sneakers squeaked on the polished tiles. "I had nothing to do with the theft."

He had the grace to act ashamed. "I'm sorry." He ran a hand over his balding head, smoothing stray wisps. "I'm beside myself, to be honest. This is going to ruin us. And not merely the museum—the whole island."

"Hopefully you'll get her back," Penny said.

Barry's expression remained gloomy. "I hope so. And that she's intact." He seemed to realize he was being remiss in his duties as docent.

"Is there anything I can help you with?"

"Not really," Penny said. "I guess I wanted to see for myself that she is really gone."

"I keep checking myself," Barry said wryly. "Thinking maybe it's nothing more than a bad dream." He came around the end of the counter, and together they walked into the exhibit room. "Unfortunately, I'm shocked afresh each time."

The case was indeed empty, a disturbing sight. Penny could understand the sense of violation Barry must have felt upon discovering the theft. The descriptive captions remained on the wall, and she scanned one detailing the discovery of the Lady. "'Professor Horace Danvers,'" she read aloud, recalling something Barry had mentioned on her first visit to the museum. "He was your ancestor, right?"

Barry beamed with pride. "He was indeed. It was his work that led to the discovery of the Lady. He saved her from being destroyed by zealous locals harvesting peat."

Seeing Barry's familial pride gave Penny a deeper understanding of the man. The museum was more than his passion project. It represented his family legacy. Sadly, the Lady was truly irreplaceable.

"Not many bog bodies have been found, have they?" Penny asked. "I wonder how many have been ruined over the centuries."

"To be fair, it's understandable," Barry said. "It's not the kind of thing you expect to find when you're digging up peat. Plus, the tannins turn everything the same color so it's really easy to overlook bodies."

"She was a real miracle find," Penny said. "Amazing. I sincerely hope she's returned soon."

"Thank you." Barry dipped his head in acknowledgment. "Miss—"

"Cavanagh. Call me Penny."

"I have a booklet I'm going to gift you since you're so interested in my ancestor's discovery."

"I'd like that," Penny said as she followed Barry out to the lobby. He flipped through a rack and gave her the pamphlet, which was about twenty pages long with illustrations included. "Here you are."

"Thank you." Penny tucked the booklet into her handbag. "I'd better run. We're camping out on the small island tonight." Right after she said that, she could have bitten her tongue. It was better that people didn't know that they were leaving the caravans unattended. Granted, with Carroll transporting the dig team by boat, the whole village was probably aware of their every move.

Barry was already shuffling papers behind the counter. "Have a nice day, Miss—er, Penny. See you soon."

"You too, Barry." As Penny left the museum, she realized she felt sorry for the man. He was right to be fearful about the future of the museum without its main attraction.

Unless the archaeological team made another groundbreaking discovery. Finding a hoard of gold would put Anoach Island on the map for sure, especially in an age when such news could easily go viral.

As Penny climbed into Nora's car, another vehicle pulled in. To her surprise, Lee was at the wheel. Last she knew, he had been holed up in his caravan, too sick to go anywhere.

Penny waited until he pulled into a space and shut off the engine, then she walked over. "Hey, Lee," she said when she reached his open car window.

He startled. "Penny."

"Glad to see you're feeling better."

He began fiddling with his belongings on the passenger seat—a messenger bag, a tablet, and several books. "You probably wonder what I'm up to."

"Not exactly," Penny said, even though she was dying of curiosity.

"It's good to see you're up and around. You're coming to Beag Anoach with me, right?"

Lee answered with a sigh. He grabbed his messenger bag and opened his door, forcing her to step aside. "I'm not sure." He shut the door, looming over her, and finally said, "I'm working on something. Something big."

"To do with the hoard?" Penny guessed. Maybe he had leads as to what could be buried at the site. In that case, she wasn't sure why he'd fake an illness. She was pretty sure Oliver would welcome the investigation.

"No, not the hoard." Lee settled the messenger bag strap on his shoulder. "The Lady. I think she's a fake."

11

Lee's words echoed in Penny's mind as she continued on to the general store. What did he mean, exactly? Was it possible someone had created a fake bog body? That would be a good reason not to have her analyzed. *Specimen identified as horse hair*, she imagined a lab reporting. If Lee was right, how did he know without seeing or examining the body? Had *he* stolen her?

"Good morning. How can I help you?" Muriel Gleason asked in a flat tone.

Penny peered at the storekeeper. Muriel didn't look well, her eyes red-rimmed and her hair standing on end. Penny thought of inquiring, but she didn't want to be intrusive.

Fishing around in her bag, Penny found her shopping list. "I've got quite a list today. Supplies for our camping trip." Muriel must be aware of the planned campout since her son had transported Oliver, Paige, and Nora out to the island.

"I'll help you put it together." Muriel came around the counter and grabbed one of the few shopping carts.

Penny was surprised at her offer but glad for the assistance. Muriel knew where everything was in the store's eclectic shelving system.

"Did you hear about the Lady?" Muriel asked. "What a loss."

For an instant, Penny wondered if she was referring to Caroline or the bog body. The body, she decided. "It is. I actually came here from the museum. Barry is pretty upset."

"We all are." Muriel gestured toward a rack of Lady of the Bog gift items. "She's a big draw. First thing people want to see when they arrive on the island."

"Any theories?" Penny asked, thinking Muriel's ideas might reflect those of the islanders in general.

Muriel stopped the cart in front of the canned goods, which were tucked next to the fishing vests and hats. "I don't think it was you dig folks, though Barry was convinced at first. I know that archaeologists like to do everything by the book. Theft in the dead of night isn't your style."

"Thanks," Penny said, surprised by the vote of confidence. "Who else would take it?"

Muriel glanced around before lowering her voice. "I think it was people from Dungsley who did it. Everyone wants the bog body for themselves."

"Dungsley?" The name rang a bell. "You mean the village before the causeway?" Penny remembered chatting with the man at the gas station. He'd mentioned the Lady of the Bog.

"Exactly." Muriel's eyes gleamed with anger. "They claim that the Lady was found in a Dungsley bog. No such luck, I tell 'em. She was found here and belongs here."

"So you think they took her and will stage a discovery?" Penny asked. The whole notion sounded absurd to her. However, she had witnessed the passion the ancient Lady inspired.

Muriel flapped a hand. "I don't know what those nitwits will do. I think they're jealous of us and always have been. The Lady brings thousands of people here every year."

"Did you tell the Garda your theory?" Penny asked.

Muriel made a scoffing noise. "The Lady is a low priority to them. I already brought it up when they came into the store. The DI merely said, 'Very interesting.' Not much support there."

Conversation tapered off as they continued shopping. Penny found almost everything on her list, quickly deciding on substitutions for the one or two items lacking. Muriel added the order to the dig's account while Carroll loaded everything into crates and took them out to the car.

When Corky started barking, Penny hastily said goodbye to Muriel and hurried outside. "Cut it out, Corky," she commanded. "Sorry about that, Carroll." She unlocked the rear hatch. "Thanks for everything."

"No problem." Carroll easily hefted the crates into the back, then shut the hatch. "All set?"

"I am, thanks. I'll be taking the small boat out myself, so wish me luck." With the task almost upon her, Penny was starting to feel nervous.

"You'll be fine," he said. "The water is calm today. Remember, don't get yourself broadside to a roller. Flip you right over, it will."

"Thanks for the warning." Penny cemented the advice about avoiding taking a wave to the side of the boat in her mind. She knew not to do that in a canoe or kayak, but she hadn't registered that a motorboat might be as easily capsized.

Carroll shifted his feet. "So, did you folks find anything interesting out on Beag?"

Penny knew what he meant. He'd already asked Paige about gold. "That's a question for Oliver," she said, forcing down her annoyance. "I'm the cook. And on that note, I'd better get going. People will be waiting for their lunch."

As Penny backed out and pulled away, she noticed that Carroll loitered outside the store, watching her. It wasn't a comfortable position to know secrets, and her answer had probably been more revealing than not. If there was a hoard, she hoped they would find it soon, before someone else did—or, at the very least, made things difficult by trying.

Lee's car was at the caravan park, so after putting Corky inside her caravan and giving the pup a snack, Penny went to knock on Lee's door. She heard shuffling and footsteps, and then the door opened.

"Hey, Penny," he said. "Come on in. I'll be ready in a few."

The caravan was almost identical to the one she and Nora were in. Lee's living room sofa was stacked with books, folders, and papers, with a slim laptop set to one side. He'd probably been working.

"You're going with me to Beag Anoach?" she confirmed.

"I am." Lee went over to the couch and closed the laptop. "I figure I can keep working online out there."

"If we get a signal," Penny pointed out.

"Yeah, if we do." Lee began winding the laptop cord. "You're probably wondering what I was talking about earlier." He paused. "I'm not sure why I'm telling you this."

"People confide in me all the time." Penny shrugged. "I used to be a matchmaker, so it must be something about my demeanor."

Lee's brows lifted. "Really? Bet you have all kinds of stories."

Penny chuckled. "Sure do."

"Anyway," Lee went on. "You know that most bog bodies have been discovered in Scandinavia and Germany, right? Some in Ireland and England as well."

"So the Lady isn't the only Irish one?" Penny perched on an overstuffed armchair.

"No, although a number have been lost over the years, some even reburied. The Lady was by far the best, most complete specimen."

Penny wondered where he was going with his theory. If the Lady had been the sole Irish bog body, she'd see a reason for his skepticism.

"To recap, it's not the location that's an issue for me," Lee said. "It's the steadfast refusal of Barry Danvers and previous holders of the body that sparked my suspicions. None of the proposed tests would damage the body. One archaeologist even offered to bring a portable X-ray machine to study the body. That was utterly refused by Barry's father."

"That is strange," Penny said. "Barry didn't want Caroline to examine her hair either."

"Exactly." Lee sifted through his papers. "Again, that might not mean anything by itself. Then I found this." He handed Penny a photocopied newspaper article, dated 1903.

Archaeologist Questioned in Hoax, the headline read. Penny scanned the text quickly. A professor by the name of Clarence Osgood had been asked about Greek jewelry found in Russia and later discovered to be fake. The Louvre had bought the pieces, which was embarrassing for them. Osgood claimed that he had left the site by the time the jewelry was discovered.

"Different dig, different continent, I realize," Lee said. "But it's interesting to me that Osgood, who was with Danvers when they found the Lady, was under suspicion at all."

"Have there been a lot of archaeological forgeries?" Penny asked.

"A fair number," Lee said. "It's harder now with the advances in scientific analysis. Piltdown Man, the supposed link between man and apes, is one example. That skeleton was a mix of human and orangutan bones."

"Why do people do it?" Penny asked. Then she answered her own question. "Money, fame, credibility—never mind. I get it. In this case, a whole economy is built around the Lady. Muriel Gleason is upset about the impact on her business."

Lee's expression sobered. "I understand that. However, the truth needs to come out. There will be no one happier than me if the Lady is genuine."

Penny couldn't tell whether Lee was being sincere. Uncovering a fraud was far more newsworthy than verifying the accepted truth.

Considering Lee's explosive theory, she also wondered if Caroline's death was related to the Lady. She'd been adamant about having the body examined.

"Would strontium analysis reveal where the Lady probably spent her life?" Penny asked.

Lee nodded. "Strontium in human hair analysis is matched to the amount of the element found in the environment—rocks, soil, and water. It can give clues to where people lived." He selected a few more folders and books and stuffed them into a bag.

If the Lady wasn't from Ireland and Barry knew it, there was a solid reason for him to refuse the testing. Circumstantial evidence, perhaps, but worthy of investigation.

"If you need help tracking down information, feel free to ask," Penny offered. "I enjoy research."

Lee smiled. "I might take you up on that. Without the Lady to examine, we can't go very far. I'm focusing on background information right now." He glanced around. "Give me a few more minutes to throw some clothes together, and then I'll help you load the boat."

"Thanks, Lee." Penny was glad to have him along. If something went wrong on the way over, at least another capable adult would be present.

As she exited the caravan, she decided to double-check the kitchen supplies. Lost in thought, she almost crashed into Carroll Gleason at the bottom of the steps.

"Whoa." She put up her hands. "Sorry."

He took a step back, a crooked grin on his face. "Didn't mean to scare you." He pointed at the caravan. "Is Lee inside?"

"Yes. He's packing for our trip." As she headed away and Carroll knocked on the door, she wondered what the two men had to discuss.

She also wondered if Carroll had been listening to their conversation and asked about Lee's presence to hide that. All the windows were wide open, and, in fact, she could hear their voices from where she stood. With a shake of her head, Penny kept going. She didn't have time to eavesdrop.

Penny checked the crates she'd packed with pots and pans, cooking utensils, paper goods, and eating utensils, deciding she had everything. It was time to load the boat and get over to Beag Anoach.

A tiny neon-green car made its way down the lane to the parking lot. Instead of stopping there, it continued on to a caravan that Penny knew was empty. New renters?

Out of curiosity, she watched as the car stopped and a woman emerged from the driver's side. It took a moment for her to recognize Kinzi Eagan. The woman wore jeans, a sweatshirt, and sneakers instead of a cloak.

As Penny crossed the grass to say hello, Kinzi went around to the hatchback and opened it. She pulled out a tray holding a variety of cleaners and tools.

"Hello, Kinzi," Penny greeted her. When Kinzi regarded her blankly, Penny went on, "We met on the beach the other day. I was with another woman and a dog." She didn't bother to mention that Kinzi had come to Caroline's caravan to confront Oliver while Penny was there.

Recognition dawned in Kinzi's eyes. "That's right." She set down the tray and reached inside again, retrieving a small vacuum cleaner.

"Are you staying here?" Penny asked. "I'm in that caravan over there." She pointed.

"Not me," Kinzi said. "I'm here to clean. A new renter is coming in."

Penny realized that the Gleasons must have hired Kinzi as a cleaner to keep the caravans up to snuff. That made sense since they were so busy with the store and transporting people around.

"Do you have a cleaning business?" Penny asked, trying to keep conversation flowing enough to eventually ask about the theft of the Lady. Considering her obsession, Kinzi might know something helpful.

"I do," Kinzi said. "I clean all kinds of places. It's grand because I work for myself and set my own schedule. Well, within reason. Got to keep my clients happy." Tote in one hand, vacuum in the other, she started toward the caravan door.

"It's pretty upsetting about the Lady, isn't it?" Penny blurted. "I was shocked."

Kinzi turned around slowly. "They shouldn't have dug her up in the first place. It was sacrilegious and disrespectful." Spots of color flamed in her cheeks. "If the Lady was your ancestor, wouldn't you think she deserved a proper burial?"

Penny couldn't argue with that point, so she didn't try. She noticed Lee stepping out of his caravan, so she left Kinzi to go about her business and went to meet Lee.

Once everything was loaded in the small boat, Lee offered to pilot it across.

Although tempted, Penny knew she was simply shifting the challenge to another day. "Thanks, but I'll do it," she said. "It's important for me to practice, in case I need to ferry people around or come back for supplies."

"Suit yourself." Lee settled on the bench seat, surrounded by piles of gear and Corky. He and the dog watched closely as Penny went through the steps to start the boat motor.

"Do you two have to stare at me?" she muttered when the motor failed to catch. She felt flustered and fumble fingered.

Lee grinned. "Not much else to look at."

Attempting to ignore their gazes, Penny tried again, finally rewarded by the engine sputtering to life. She made an adjustment, and it smoothed out beautifully.

"Good job," Lee said.

Penny chuckled. "Thanks." She took the rudder and began steering them out of the cove on the route she'd become familiar with over the last few days. Straight across, then southeast around the island to the sheltered harbor on one end.

To her relief, the water outside the cove was calm, the waves rippling and sparkling in the sunshine. No rollers to worry about.

"Hit it," Lee called, indicating she should speed up.

Did she dare? Penny decided she would go a little faster. The boat zipped along, wind whipping through her hair. Corky loved it too, leaning out into the breeze with his fur blowing back. She exchanged an amused glance with Lee.

Within fifteen minutes, they were approaching the harbor. Penny slowed the motor to a trolling speed. When they got close to shore, she cut it entirely and drifted up to the small dock.

"That was really nice." Lee reached out and grabbed the piling, pulling the boat alongside the dock. He quickly wound the mooring line around and cleated it.

"Thanks," Penny said, pleased. If she didn't have work to do, she would love to take the boat for a longer ride. There was such freedom in being out on the water.

"I'll get Oliver to come help," Lee said, grabbing a couple of crates. "Don't hurt yourself lugging stuff."

"I won't," Penny said. After leashing Corky so he wouldn't run off to explore again, she selected the lightest crate. Lee's idea about an all-terrain vehicle made more sense every day.

Penny's phone rang when she was halfway up the hill. She almost let it go to voice mail, then realized it might be the Garda.

"Hold on, Corky," she said as he continued to pull. She set the crate down and fished around for her phone. *Where is it?* She found it at the bottom of her handbag. "Hello?" she answered quickly, not bothering to check the caller identification.

"Ms. Cavanagh?" A woman's voice. "This is DI Babcock."

"Hello, Detective Inspector. I'm so glad you called. Did you find the car?"

A pause. "I'm afraid not. The barn was empty."

Penny's heart sank. "Did you have the right barn? I couldn't find a road name."

"It was the same barn. The island isn't all that large."

Penny's mind raced. "They must have moved the car." Had someone seen her lurking around the barn? She swayed on her feet. What if they had accosted her and tried to prevent her from reporting the crime? *Talk about a close call.*

"Are you all right, Ms. Cavanagh? You made an odd sound."

Penny blinked. "I think so." She forced herself to take a couple of deep breaths. "Someone must have seen me at the barn. The idea scared me."

"How did you find the barn in the first place?"

Penny thought she'd mentioned the circumstances in her message, but the Garda liked to go over details more than once. "On complete accident, actually. I had my cousin's dog with me. He was whining, so I pulled over to let him out. He took off for the barn, and when I went to find him, I saw the car."

"What made you think it was involved in the hit-and-run?" The DI likely wanted to know why Penny had examined the car in the first place.

"Besides the dents, you mean? I visited Kenneth in the hospital the other day, and he said he caught a flash of red. When I found a red car parked in a barn, I immediately thought of him, so I checked the front fenders. You saw the pictures." She thought of something else that was suspicious. "There were no number plates. I found that odd."

"Not if someone took it off the road."

"True." However, Penny still had the feeling that the red car had hit Kenneth. Aware from experience that the Garda didn't put any stock in feelings, however, she said, "I hope you find the person who hit Kenneth soon, and that you didn't mind me passing along the information."

"Certainly not," Babcock said. "Please continue to contact me with anything that might be relevant. Including about Caroline Pierce's death." She made an amused sound. "I checked into your Detective Inspector Campbell and came across some very interesting stories about you, Ms. Cavanagh. You have a knack for investigation, it seems."

"All purely accidental," Penny said. "Mysteries find me. I don't go looking for them." Did she have anything to share regarding Caroline's death? The bog body had been stolen after Caroline died and was no longer a threat to the specimen. She'd clashed with Oliver, which the Garda already knew. The visit with Kenneth came into her mind.

"Kenneth told me that Caroline was a very difficult person," Penny said. When Babcock didn't respond, she added, "I know that's not much to go on."

"It isn't, really," Babcock said. "Whenever there are too few top spots and too many people who want to fill them, you get professional rivalry and all kinds of conflicts."

"Kenneth also told us that the island was Caroline's 'old stomping grounds.' That she had family here. It was news to Nora, my cousin. She met Caroline when they were at university."

"She did have family here," Babcock said. "You may have met them. Muriel and Carroll Gleason."

12

"The Gleasons?" Penny wasn't sure how to voice her confusion. Surely as relatives, they should have been more involved in the investigation, more grieved by Caroline's death. Muriel hadn't said a word about it when Penny was with her in the store.

"It's a distant connection," Babcock said. "That's all I can say about it."

"Of course," Penny said. "Thank you, Detective Inspector."

"Thank you, Ms. Cavanagh." Babcock hung up.

Penny pondered the new information as she trudged toward the dig site. Caroline had family on Anoach Island. While it sounded as if she'd had minimal contact with them, it begged the question: Did Caroline's death have to do with something in her family history?

She met Lee and Oliver as she headed down the slope. "Thought you got lost," Lee said.

"I had a phone call." Penny tugged Corky's leash gently, drawing his attention away from the clump of grass he was sniffing. "Come on, boy."

"We'll get the rest of the stuff," Oliver offered.

Grateful for their help, Penny went straight to the dining area. Several camping tents had been put up at the edge of the dig area. Paige and Nora were working in a trench, and they waved in greeting.

After filling Corky's water dish, Penny organized the meal preparation area. Oliver and Lee soon appeared with the rest of the food and cooking supplies.

"I'll make sandwiches for lunch," Penny said. "Ready for a break?"

"We are." Oliver checked his watch. "Ten minutes? Lee is going to get his sleeping bag and clothes. I'm glad to see he's recovered from whatever it was."

Playing truant. Penny didn't say that, though. "Me too. Working the dig is even harder down a person, isn't it?"

"Yet another person, you mean." Oliver surveyed the site. "We need to take advantage of the good weather."

Glad that Oliver seemed comfortable stepping in as de facto supervisor until the higher ups could decide what to do about the team's losses, Penny studied the clear blue sky. "Is bad weather in the forecast?"

"Not right now," Oliver said. "Storms develop suddenly in the summer sometimes, especially when it's this hot and humid."

He wandered off and Penny started making roast beef sandwiches. After that day's lunch, the menu would be peanut butter and jelly or canned tuna, both nonperishable. She had bought vacuum-sealed mayonnaise packets that didn't need to be refrigerated. Potato chips and carrot and celery sticks rounded out the simple meal.

"Lunch is ready," she called, amusing herself with a wish that she had brought the kind of triangle used on ranches to summon workers to their meals.

The team straggled over, and soon everyone was seated under the tarp. "I'm glad to see you made it out here all right, Penny," Nora said. "How did the boat handle?"

"It was fine," Penny said. "The water is calm today."

"We were pretty loaded down with me along," Lee put in. "Penny did great." Anxiety lurked in his eyes, making Penny think he was worried what she would tell the others about his fake illness.

It wasn't up to her to tell tales on Lee. If Oliver wasn't happy with Lee's performance at the dig, he'd have to take it up with him. "I was glad to have your help," Penny said. "By the way, I learned something interesting today when I spoke to Detective Inspector Babcock."

"Detective Inspector Babcock?" Paige repeated sharply. "What were you talking to her about?"

Penny didn't want to tell anyone except Nora about the red car in the barn, so she said, "Nothing, really. Touching base. She mentioned that Caroline is related to the Gleasons."

Oliver's eyebrows shot up. "As in Muriel and Carroll Gleason?"

"Exactly," Penny said. "It surprised me too."

"You didn't know that, Oliver?" Paige asked, disbelief heavy in her voice. "You were married to her."

Oliver shook his head. "She didn't talk about her family much. A couple vague remarks about cousins in western Ireland, that's all. Since she didn't give them any importance, neither did I."

Nora appeared thoughtful. "Did any of you see Caroline talking to Carroll? I didn't."

Everyone shook their heads. "She didn't even acknowledge him when he brought us to the island or when he came back with Barry," Oliver noted.

"That is pretty rude," Paige said. "I wouldn't be happy if one of my relatives did that to me." She bit into a chip with a crunch.

Lee made a scoffing sound. "I doubt he killed her over it."

So did Penny. Unless there was a deep and festering rift between branches of the family and Carroll had snapped. "It's a possible area of inquiry."

"Listen to you." Paige laughed. "You sound like a proper investigator."

"She's solved quite a few cases," Oliver said. "I hear she's good at it."

Penny cringed. She wished people wouldn't talk about her investigations, especially while there was an unsolved murder staring them in the face. For all she knew, the person who had pushed Caroline off the cliff was sitting among them at that very moment. "Not on purpose. Somehow I always seem to stumble onto clues."

"Sounds like our work," Lee said.

"We don't *stumble* onto finds," Paige said, offended. "It's all methodical and carefully thought out."

"Most of the time," Oliver said. "I didn't expect to find that gold coin." He ate the last corner of his sandwich. "And on that note, let's get back to work."

They made good headway that afternoon. With everyone working in the same area and both Penny and Nora sifting, they were able to double their typical progress.

"Quick break for dinner and then keep going?" Oliver pushed his trowel into the earth beside the trench. "It doesn't get dark until nine."

A few groans escaped before the other archaeologists agreed.

"I can put together a quick chicken chili," Penny offered. She would use canned goods for simplicity's sake. "Ready in twenty minutes."

"Make it thirty," Oliver said. "Take a break yourself, Penny. If we get in a couple more hours tonight, that will be fine."

Penny washed her face and hands with tepid water and soap before putting the meal together. She mixed everything in a large pan and set it to simmer on the camping stove.

Nora appeared in the dining area with Corky on a leash. "Want to take a quick walk, Penny?"

Lee arrived too, holding an electronic tablet and his phone. "I'll watch the food, Penny. I'm on the trail of some very interesting information about our archaeologists."

"What do you mean?" Nora asked.

"He's checking into the men who discovered the Lady," Penny said. "One of them was Barry Danvers's ancestor. That's one reason why he's so protective of her."

"Makes sense," Nora said. "Family reputation and all that."

"Exactly." Penny checked the flame one more time. "Give the pot a stir every couple of minutes, will you, Lee?"

After he agreed, Penny and Nora set off toward the shore, a happy dog bouncing along in front, behind, and beside them. Corky was all over the place.

"Wait until I tell you about my day," Penny said. "I had quite the adventure."

Nora grinned. "Why am I not surprised? Do tell."

"I'll show you." Penny pulled out her phone and brought up the pictures of the barn. "Corky and I stopped here on the way to the store."

Nora scrolled through the photos. She gave a yelp when she noticed the damaged fender. "That car probably hit Kenneth. He said he saw something red."

"That's what I thought too," Penny said. "I sent them to DI Babcock. Get this—the car was gone when they went to the barn."

"No way." Nora handed the phone back, and they strolled on. "How did the person know to move the car?"

"That's a very good question," Penny said. "And I don't like the answer. They must have spotted me poking around."

"Did you see anyone on the property? Or on the road?"

"No one. It was totally deserted out there." Then she had an idea. "Maybe there was a camera in the barn."

"That's possible," Nora said. "A lot of people have them nowadays. They're not that expensive."

Penny groaned. "I hope they didn't see my face. It was pretty dark in there," she added hopefully.

Nora looked her cousin up and down. "Unfortunately, you're very distinctive. In a totally good way, I mean."

"You're probably right." Penny's shoulders slumped. "Now I'll be checking over my shoulder constantly."

"At least you're safe out here. It's us and the seabirds."

"There's more," Penny said. "After we left the barn, I stopped by the museum. I spoke to Barry for a few minutes, and that's when he told me about his ancestor. He's pretty upset over the theft, and so is Muriel."

"I don't blame them. The Lady is a huge tourist attraction."

They reached the edge of the land, which ended in a cliff. The villagers who had settled on the island had probably chosen the spot for that reason, so the settlement could be easily defended.

Penny couldn't help but think of another cliff, the spot where Caroline Pierce had met her fate. "Muriel especially seemed upset. Knowing what we do now, that Caroline was her relative, I think she was grieving."

"That's so sad," Nora said. "Poor thing."

They stood in silence for a moment, watching the seagulls swoop over the water. The afternoon was calm, and waves rippled gently on the shore below.

"Lee wasn't sick," Penny said. "He's been pretending."

Nora laughed. "I thought that might be it. What is he up to?"

"He thinks the Lady is a fake. Well, it's a real body, but it might not have come from Ireland. He wants to be the one to expose the truth."

Nora gazed thoughtfully into the distance. "That's a very interesting theory. Kind of hard to prove without the actual body, though, isn't it?"

Had someone gotten wind of Lee's quest? That was possible if he'd asked too many questions. "Do you think Barry staged the theft?" Penny asked. "His ancestor found the body."

"That would be a logical conclusion," Nora said. "Maybe he's hiding her until Lee loses steam. If Caroline is gone and Lee is stumped, the Lady will be safe."

"That makes total sense." Penny glanced at the dining canopy and noticed that Paige and Oliver had joined Lee. "Time for dinner."

Penny served bowls of chili and passed around a plate of rolls and butter. Everyone dug in, eating heartily until the last morsel was gone.

"That was great, Penny," Oliver said. "It really hit the spot after working hard all day." He grinned at his team. "Now back to the trenches. Literally."

Everyone groaned good-naturedly, then scattered to wash up before returning to work. As Penny was cleaning the dining area, Lee approached her. "I found something interesting," he said in a low voice. "Regarding the Lady."

Penny's ears perked up. While she sympathized with Barry, Muriel, and anyone else who depended upon the Lady as a tourist draw, she was curious. "A direct mention of her provenance?"

"Nothing that definitive, unfortunately. But I have learned that Professor Danvers went on expeditions to Scandinavia. He was present when a bog body was found in Denmark."

Penny put it all together in her mind. "So he had connections. He also knew where to search."

"The picture is becoming clearer," Lee said with satisfaction. "Danvers had the link to the source while his partner, Clarence Osgood, had the lack of scruples. He probably talked Danvers into the hoax. Finding the Lady solidified both their reputations as leading archaeologists of the time. They were granted all kinds of funding to work in Ireland, where they both lived."

As a theory, it held together—assuming the men were that crooked.

Means, motive, and opportunity were present. But was guilt?

"You really need the Lady to prove it, don't you?" Penny said.

"Otherwise, it's speculation."

Lee put a hand to his chest. "You wound me, Penny," he joked. "Though you're right. Unless I find documents showing the professors, one or both, making an unsanctioned trip to Denmark. There was too long a period between Danvers's first visit and when the Lady was discovered. Two years."

"What kind of documents are you searching for?"

Lee ticked off his fingers. "Ship manifests or other expense receipts for travel, correspondence where the trip might be mentioned, academic papers—things like that. Also, on the Denmark end, I'm hunting for any mention of the professors. That's harder, since I don't speak the language."

"Too bad you don't have the Lady," Penny noted again. "As you said, strontium tests would reveal where she came from." Surely that would be a shortcut to the truth.

"They would." Lee's eyes narrowed. "I doubt it's a coincidence she went missing right after I started asking questions."

"I was thinking that too," Penny said. "Barry gave me a pamphlet about the discovery and his ancestor that might have helpful information. Do you have a copy?"

"No." Lee rested his hands on his hips. "He told me they were all gone."

Penny laughed. "You can have mine. It's in my handbag."

"I'd appreciate it," Lee said. "Anyway, I wanted to give you the update since you were so good about not ratting me out."

"It's not my business," Penny said lightly as she finished washing the last bowl. "It's between you and Oliver." She noticed that the others were gathering by the trench. "We'd better go."

Penny was taking her position with the sifter when Oliver made a surprising offer. "Do you want to try digging, Penny? It might be a nice change of pace."

Her heart leaped. "Really? I'd love it."

"Climb down in," he said. "We'll sift the buckets tomorrow, in the daylight."

Penny slid into the trench, the edges of which came up to her thighs.

Oliver handed her a trowel, dustpan, and brush, then led her to a spot. "This is your area. Examine the soil carefully, and then empty your dustpan in the bucket."

Everyone was assigned a spot and soon the only sound was the gentle scrape of trowels on the ground as they teased up another slim layer of soil.

After about an hour of the almost mindless yet soothing task, Penny's trowel scraped along a curved edge. She picked up her brush and whisked the soil away. Something was definitely there. A rock? Or something more interesting?

She didn't say anything yet, preferring to investigate further. The next tool she picked up was a skewer, the pointed tip used to dig around the outline of objects.

Penny soon realized that the rounded item stuck in the dirt wasn't a rock. It was a clay vessel measuring about a foot in length. At first, she thought she'd found pieces, which were quite common. But as she continued to define the object with her tools, she felt a leap of hope. Maybe it was intact.

"I've found something," she called. "A clay vessel."

Oliver hurried over, and she moved aside to let him inspect the object. "Very good, Penny. With any luck, it's not broken."

Penny let Oliver and Paige take over, content to watch as they skillfully teased away the soil enclosing the pot.

"What a thrill," Nora said. She and Lee had given up all pretense of work to watch.

Oliver brushed away soil at the mouth of the pot and gasped. Between two fingers, he held up a gold coin.

"Here's another one," Paige said, her voice breaking in excitement. "And another!"

Lee put a hand on Penny's shoulder. "You've done it," he said. "You've found the hoard."

13

Oliver set up battery-powered lights so they could keep working past sunset. When the rest of the clay urn was freed from the soil, they discovered it held hundreds of gold coins.

"This is a major find," Oliver said, exultant. "One of the larger hoards discovered in this part of Europe."

Penny couldn't hold back a whoop of excitement. "Wow. And to think I dug it up. Only because I was in that spot, but still." Although she expected some disgruntlement that she, an amateur, had discovered the urn, the others took it in stride and congratulated her.

Nora threw her arms around Penny. "What a story we'll have to tell."

In addition to tales of murder and theft. The discovery of gold was much more fun to discuss. "What's next?" Penny asked.

"It's quite a process," Oliver said. "We need to notify the authorities that we've discovered treasure. They'll come out here and inspect the site, and then the coins will be moved to a secure location."

Penny wished they could come that night. She suddenly felt very isolated and vulnerable out on the small island. "Are we going to guard the find until then?"

"I don't think—" Oliver started.

Lee interrupted him. "She's got a point. Carroll mentioned a hoard when he was out here. Who knows how many other villagers are keeping an eye on the dig? It would be our luck that someone comes over tonight and pokes around."

"We'll sit up in shifts," Paige said. "Two at a time. Penny, make some very strong tea. One night of poor sleep is worth it."

Oliver glanced around the site, at the moon rising over the horizon. "You're right, Lee. Better safe than sorry. Paige, why don't you and I take the first shift? We'll go until two o'clock, then Nora and Lee from two until six. Penny, you're on in the morning with me."

"Corky will be our watchdog too," Nora said.

"That will help," Oliver said. "At least he'll provide an early warning signal."

Penny clambered out of the trench, reluctant to leave her discovery behind. She'd never forget the thrill of finding an ancient vessel and then discovering it held rare gold coins. She pulled out her phone, thinking she would text Finn.

"I don't need to remind any of you," Oliver said, still in the trench. "No mentions in calls, texts, or social media until these coins are safely in custody. You know the drill."

Sheepishly, Penny put her phone back in her pocket, hoping he hadn't seen her. Of course she shouldn't tell anyone, not even the incredibly trustworthy Finn. The sole way to be sure nothing leaked was a complete communication blackout.

"I am going to place a couple of calls tonight," Oliver said. "That will provide a time marker of the discovery. No details obviously, if I have to leave messages."

Glad the precious find was in someone else's capable hands, Penny went to the dining area to wash her hands and make tea. She put the kettle on the stove and rooted through a crate for two vacuum bottles she'd brought. They would keep the tea hot during the overnight hours while people kept watch.

Paige strode into the dining area. "That was amazing, Penny. Great work for your first time digging."

"Beginner's luck, right?" Penny said. "It was simple chance that I was in that area. Oliver assigned me."

"Probably cursing his luck now." Penny must have looked aghast because Paige said, "I'm kidding. We're all going to get credit for the find, don't worry."

Penny opened the box of tea bags. "I don't want credit. This isn't my profession."

"How about your name in the paper?" Paige popped open a tin of biscuits and selected one. "There will be lots of interviews. Maybe even on television."

Penny grimaced. "I hope not."

"Not a publicity hound? Don't blame you." Paige collapsed into a folding chair. "Normally I'd dread taking the night shift, but tonight I'm too cranked up to sleep. The Beag Anoach hoard. I always thought it was a legend."

Penny set out a line of mugs. "An official legend? By that, I mean passed down through time. Not something imagined by Carroll and other locals." The rumor of treasure often circulated around any historic place, whether a building or an archaeological site.

"There are plenty of stories. My grandmother's best friend used to tell them to me." Paige took another biscuit. "I think that's why I became interested in archaeology in the first place. She really brought it all to life."

"What did the stories say about Beag Anoach?" Penny asked, fascinated.

"That a princess lived here on this headland, the civilization's guardian after her father was killed in a Viking raid. She hid the village's wealth when another raid came and they all had to flee."

"Was that the Lady?" Penny asked. Did an ancient legend support the bog body?

"The Lady was earlier, around 200 AD. The Vikings started raiding around 800 AD," Paige explained. "Naturally, the locals consider the Lady as an ancestor of the princess who hid the hoard. It makes sense. Her clothing shows high status."

When the kettle began to whistle, Penny switched off the gas, then filled the mugs and a vacuum bottle. "I've made a thermos for you and Oliver. What would you like in it?"

"A little milk," Paige said. "We can add our own sugar." She watched Penny add the milk and cap the jug. "That was thoughtful of you."

"Take the tin of biscuits too. I bought more."

Once the watch team was all set, Penny carried two mugs to her tent. Nora had the flaps open and was arranging things inside.

"Tea?" Penny asked.

Nora backed out of the tent. "I'd love some, thanks." She accepted the mug, then sat cross-legged on the ground and took a sip. "Wow. What an exciting night. I'm on cloud nine."

"So am I," Penny admitted, sitting beside Nora. Through the open doorway, she could see the two sleeping bags lined up side by side. "Thanks for setting up the tent."

"No problem. You were lugging groceries out here." Nora tossed a stick for Corky to fetch. With a happy bark, he ran to get it.

"Make sure that's really a stick," Penny joked. "Around a dig, you never know."

Nora took the stick from Corky and peered closely at it. "Yup, just a stick," she reported, and threw it again.

"Can you imagine giving a rare artifact to a dog to play with?" Penny asked rhetorically. "The handle of a tool, for instance."

"It's true that many artifacts have been plowed up, run over, or tossed away," Nora said.

"At first, I thought I'd found a rock," Penny said. "I had to keep digging before I realized it was pottery. I'm glad I didn't damage it." She would relive the moments again and again.

"Wait until Nan hears about this," Nora said with a chuckle. "She'll tell all of Blarney Green."

Penny could picture their grandmother happily sharing the tale. "That's why we can't say anything yet, though I'm dying to." Especially to Finn. She shared everything with him.

Nora yawned. "I'd better get to bed. Two in the morning is going to come quickly."

Corky's inquisitive nose woke Penny. "Corky, you goof," she grumbled, nudging him away.

"Corky, come out of there," Nora commanded sternly.

The dog retreated, and Penny sat up. Through the open flap, she saw it was morning. "What time is it?"

"Shortly after six," Nora said. "Sorry he woke you."

"I need to get up anyway." Penny unzipped her sleeping bag. "Anything happen on watch?"

"Not a thing," Nora said. "Lee and I ended up playing word games to stay awake. The best thing about it was watching the sunrise. It was really gorgeous."

"I bet." Penny tugged on a pair of sweatpants and a fleece jacket to ward off the chill in the morning air. An exciting day lay ahead, and she wanted to make a good breakfast to fuel everyone.

As she crossed the camping area to the dining canopy, Oliver emerged from his tent, phone to his ear. "We'll expect you before noon, then." He hung up. "Officials are on their way, flying out of Dublin."

That made sense. It had taken most of the day for Penny and Nora to reach the western side of the island by car.

One cooler held the few perishables Penny had brought. After putting the kettle on, she pulled out a package of bacon and placed the strips in a frying pan. "Scrambled eggs and bacon sound good?"

"Excellent." Oliver rubbed his hands together. "What a day. I barely slept a wink. I can catch up later, once the hoard is safely away."

As the bacon began to sizzle, Penny cracked eggs into a bowl. When the kettle boiled, she prepared mugs of tea.

If not for the location, a lovely island off the coast, and the rather primitive cooking setup, Penny felt as much in her element as at the tearoom. Earlier in life, she never would have guessed she'd find fulfillment in feeding people. She was finding that full bellies and happy smiles were a satisfying reward for her efforts.

"Something smells good," Lee said as he approached. "I'm going to tuck in and then crash for a while, if that's okay."

"Go for it," Oliver said from his seat at the table, where he was tapping away at his phone. "We won't have company until about noon. Our department head is pretty happy."

"I bet," Lee said. "Maybe you'll get a promotion after all."

"That'd be nice," Oliver said, still working. "I'll have Penny to thank."

Paige was last to arrive, hair braided and light makeup adorning her features. Penny glanced down at her lounge clothes. She ought to change into something more appropriate before visitors arrived, in case there were photographs.

"I have a question, Oliver." Paige pulled out a chair. "Do you think they'll want you to go back to the mainland with the hoard? I imagine there will be all kinds of meetings."

Oliver set his phone down. "You're probably right. For one thing,

I want to make sure that they get all the facts straight. Hard to do that from a distance."

Penny removed the bacon from the pan and placed it on a paper towel-covered plate. What would Oliver's absence mean for the dig?

"If you go, where does that leave us?" Lee asked, voicing Penny's question. He added sugar to his tea.

"I don't want to stop the dig, if that's what you're asking," Oliver said. "I'll be back in a day or two at the most. Once the find is logged, it will be out of my hands."

"Where do you report the find?" Penny asked. She wasn't clear about the process.

"The National Museum of Ireland," Oliver said. "The law requires treasure to be reported within ninety-six hours. They'll supervise where the items end up. We'll get a reward eventually. The university will, I mean."

"I thought treasure hunters could keep their finds and sell them," Penny said.

"In some cases," Oliver explained. "Depends on the rules of the governing authority. Here, you'd have to break the law to do that."

Paige tossed her braid. "Oliver always does things by the rules." She smiled. "As he should."

"You do if you want to keep your funding," Oliver said. "Not to mention your reputation."

Penny didn't have to be told how important a researcher's reputation was to their career. One misstep could be ruinous. She suddenly felt relief that her main concerns were frying bacon and washing dishes. *That*, she thought wryly, *and figuring out who killed Caroline, who stole the Lady of the Bog, who hit Kenneth, and what catastrophe might strike next.*

By late morning, Penny heard boats buzzing in the bay. "They're coming here," Penny told Nora when their course became apparent. The cousins were on the island's highest point of land, where they'd taken Corky for a walk. "It's too early for the authorities, right?"

"Word about the find must have leaked," Nora said with a huff.

"I wonder how."

"I certainly haven't told anyone, and you would think that Paige and Lee are professional enough not to, either." Penny groaned as it clicked. "If Oliver arranged for Carroll to bring government employees out, that would give it away."

Nora whistled to Corky, who was straying along a path heading down the wrong way. "It sure would. And if Carroll told Muriel—"

"The whole island knows." Penny didn't fault anyone for spreading the news. The hoard had to be the most exciting discovery in the area since the Lady, found over a century earlier.

Penny and Nora remained on their hilltop, watching as boats landed and people climbed out. "Oliver is going to need crowd control," Penny noted.

"We should probably warn him." Nora pulled out her phone and checked for a signal. "I think a call will go through." She dialed and put the phone on speaker.

"Nora? Are you okay?" Oliver asked.

"We're fine," Nora assured him. "We're up on the hill with Corky. Listen, you're about to get inundated with visitors. Maybe you should have the Garda come out here and help."

"Seriously?" Oliver groaned. "I heard the boats, but I didn't realize what it meant. I'll call them right away. Thanks for the tip."

Nora slid her phone back into her jacket pocket and zipped it up, then she leaned against a tall boulder and pulled a folded paper from another pocket.

"What's that?" Penny asked as Nora unfolded the page.

"A map of this island. Want to see?"

Penny joined Nora at the boulder. Corky sprawled in the long grass nearby.

Nora pointed out different features on the map. "This is where we are. That's the path to the dig. The path that Corky almost took goes down to another cove."

"It looks like there's a beach." Penny tapped a tiny seashell emblem. "Maybe we can explore it sometime." She peered closer at the map, trying to decipher the handwritten notations and little drawings illustrating certain points. "Where did this come from?"

"It's a copy of a very old one," Nora said. "Maybe from the 1800s? I was thinking of making my own version and illustrating the Iron Age village. I could add quaint touches, like basking sharks in the water and the Lady standing up here, gazing over the island."

Penny beamed at her cousin's talent. "You could sell them. I'm sure businesses around here would want them. The university too, for their bookstore. And the museum that ends up with the hoard."

"That's the plan," Nora said. "I'm going to approach a few presses rather than print and distribute them myself."

Penny glanced out at the bay, where two sizable vessels were now traversing the water. "Here come the Garda. And the Irish Coast Guard."

Nora laughed. "Oliver called in the troops."

Tipping her head, Penny scanned the sky.

"What are you doing?" Nora asked.

"Seeing if I can spot any helicopters. I'm surprised the news channels aren't here yet."

Nora pushed herself upright from the boulder. "Any minute now, I'm sure."

Penny's phone dinged. When she checked the screen, she saw a text from Finn.

You found treasure? Call when you can.

She shared the message with Nora, who shook her head and said, "Brace yourself. The word is definitely out."

Helicopters didn't arrive, but a few local reporters with recorders and handheld cameras did join the crowd of onlookers.

When Oliver gestured for Penny to join him at the trench with the officials, she felt a rush of relief that she'd changed into flattering jeans and one of her favorite tops. Her hair was brushed and gleaming, and she wore enough makeup to feel attractive on camera.

"Tell us how you found the urn," a reporter called after Oliver introduced Penny.

Trying not to mutter or stumble over words, Penny relayed the story: How she'd discovered the curved edge and gradually revealed the pot, and the thrill she felt when she found a gold coin. "I thought the hoard was a rumor, a myth. Now we've proved it true." She gestured toward the excavated urn, which rested in a crate packed with straw, most of the coins still inside. They would be removed and examined in a secure lab.

"Are you an archaeologist?" another reporter asked. "Where did you go to school?"

Penny felt her cheeks flush. "I'm not. This is my first dig, as an assistant. I usually make tea for a living."

Something about her honest statement struck a chord, and everyone laughed.

Oliver stepped forward. "And very good tea it is. I'll take questions."

Penny slipped away as the reporters began tossing out questions related to the find and the dig as a whole. No one was over by the dining canopy, so she thought she'd put the kettle on. The mention of tea made her realize how much she wanted a cup. Plus, she needed a break from the crowd and all the staring eyes.

As she put the kettle on, she noticed that one of the officials was being interviewed. People began to drift from the crowd, probably thinking the excitement was over. They'd seen the urn and the gold coin Oliver held up, and that had satisfied their curiosity.

Two of the onlookers strolled toward the dining area. Penny recognized Barry Danvers and Muriel Gleason. Penny imagined that, as two prominent locals, they had a greater purpose here than most.

"Any sign of the Lady yet, Barry?" Muriel asked as they approached.

Barry huffed. "Not yet. The Garda haven't been much help either. Have they any clues about your cousin's death?"

Muriel shook her head. "If they do, they haven't told me. Though they've questioned me enough."

Penny's ears perked up. She hadn't been aware that the Garda were questioning Muriel and perhaps regarded her as a suspect.

"They're merely being thorough," Barry said.

"A bit too thorough for my taste." Muriel huffed. "Apparently, they think Caroline was planning to challenge my inheritance from our grandmother."

14

"Did she?" When Penny heard the words floating on the air, she put a hand to her mouth. She hadn't meant to say them out loud.

Muriel raised an eyebrow as if surprised Penny would be so bold. "Not that I know of, lass. She never said anything to me directly."

"I wonder why they think that, though," Penny went on, figuring she'd already gone too far so why stop? Barry also seemed interested in the answer.

Muriel shrugged. "Maybe there was something among her belongings. I gave her the attorney's name when she said she needed some paperwork done."

So either the Garda had put two and two together incorrectly, or Caroline really had been planning to reopen the probate case. Either way, the Garda were exploring that avenue. Did that mean Muriel and her son were suspects?

"How were you related, exactly?" Penny asked. She might as well press her luck until it ran out.

"Caroline's mam and my mam were cousins. Once her mam moved to London, we barely ever saw her again. I met Caroline a few times. We didn't stay in touch in between, so I barely knew her."

And now they'll never have an opportunity. Penny tried to find a resemblance between Muriel and Caroline, but they looked nothing alike and were on quite different paths in life. Still, there were similarities. For instance, both women were very strong-minded.

Had they clashed? Unfortunately, Penny could imagine it all too well.

"I met her once, years ago, on one of her visits," Barry said. "I thought that common ground would make her more receptive to my point of view about disturbing the Lady." He clamped his lips together. "Alas, it did not."

"Caroline could be stubborn," Muriel said. "I remember that about her."

The kettle whistled, and Penny hastened to switch off the gas. "Cup of tea?"

Oliver, the rest of the team, and the officials joined them under the canopy to drink tea and eat biscuits. Penny made a note to buy more of both when she went ashore. The Garda and Coast Guard herded away the rest of the onlookers and press, the drone of boats announcing their departure. Muriel and Barry still lingered, chatting amiably with everyone. They even fussed over Corky, who ate up the attention.

"You should be all set now," Detective Inspector Babcock told Oliver. She had detoured to the dining area before leaving with the other gardaí.

"Thanks for coming," Oliver said. "We appreciate it."

Penny was surprised to see an officer of Babcock's level providing guard duty. Then the inspector said, "I wouldn't have missed it for the world. My little boy will be beside himself when he hears about the treasure."

"We're walking on air ourselves," Oliver said with a laugh. "It's very exciting indeed."

Babcock touched Oliver's arm, drawing him aside. "You really shouldn't leave the site unattended. I understand you're accompanying the find to Dublin."

"I am," Oliver said. "Several members of my team will be staying here while I'm gone."

"Good to hear," Babcock replied. "Otherwise, you might come back to see the entire headland all dug up by treasure hunters."

Oliver shuddered. "Heaven forbid. That would totally destroy the integrity of the site. We excavate in layers for a reason."

"So I understand," the inspector said. "I'll be on my way now, unless there is anything else."

Although Penny wanted to ask if they had any strong leads in Caroline's death or the theft of the Lady, she managed to refrain. Then she remembered the red car and hurried after Babcock. "Detective Inspector," she called, rushing to catch up.

Babcock stopped and waited. "How can I help you, Ms. Cavanagh?"

Penny lowered her voice, not wanting anyone to overhear her. "Any leads on the red car?" she asked. When the garda stared at her, she added, "Since my cousin and I found Kenneth, I'm really anxious that the driver is found." She wanted to make it clear that she wasn't meddling.

"Not yet," Babcock said, relenting. "Not that I'll inform you when we do find the driver and car."

"I understand."

Babcock pivoted on her heel and walked on.

As Penny returned to the dining area, she wondered if answers would ever come. Once again, she was up to her neck in mysteries and as mystified as ever.

When Penny arrived back at the dining area, Oliver pulled her and Nora aside. "Do you two mind staying here with Lee for another night? Paige is coming with me to Dublin. We should be back late tomorrow."

"Not at all," Nora said. "We have Corky, after all. He'll run any intruders off."

"Don't confront anyone," Oliver warned. "I've already spoken to the Garda and they'll send someone immediately. The Coast Guard is also providing backup. They patrol the bay on a regular basis. They'll make note of any craft around the island."

"So if someone does manage to steal something, they'll be tracked down and arrested?" Penny asked.

"That's the plan," Oliver said. "They'll also be arrested for trespassing if they're carrying so much as a shovel."

Under the circumstances Oliver described, Penny decided staying on the island would be all right. "As long as you leave a boat for us, we'll be fine."

"The small one will be staying here," Oliver reassured her. "Now I'd better go get ready. We need to make the flight."

Soon the group of officials, Oliver, and Paige left the site with the crated treasure, leaving a slightly forlorn atmosphere behind them. The party was over.

"It's certainly quiet now," Penny said with a sigh. She began to pick up paper cups and other detritus left in the dining area.

Nora came over to help clean up. "I think I'll do some sketching. Maybe work on my map."

Once the dining area was shipshape, Penny retreated to a spot overlooking the water with her phone. Thinking Finn might be busy, she sent a text first.

I'd love to chat if you're free.

In response, her phone rang. "Hello," she sang out. "How are you?"

"I'm fine," Finn said. "How's my favorite treasure hunter?"

Penny laughed. "Did you see me on video? I hope I didn't come off too dorky."

"You were great. A total natural."

Penny doubted that, but she accepted the compliment. After she told him the story of finding the gold, she said, "Everyone is gone now. Oliver and Paige went to Dublin with the treasure and the officials."

"So who's left on the island?" Finn asked, a concerned tone in his voice.

"Nora and Lee are here with me. Corky too. The Garda and the Coast Guard are keeping an eye on boat traffic to and from the island. We'll call them if we have any trouble."

"I hope you don't get any visitors. The news will draw treasure hunters like flies."

"Well, we found the hoard. If they want pottery shards and pieces of metal, then that's all they'll find."

"I hope they realize that. Anything else going on?"

Where to begin? "I found the car that hit Kenneth. Well, I'm almost positive it's the one. Then it disappeared."

"What? Fill me in."

Penny told Finn about discovering the red car parked in the barn due to Corky running off. She explained that she'd taken pictures and sent them to Detective Inspector Babcock, who had then informed her that the car was gone.

"That's frustrating," Finn said. "I wonder how he or she figured out you found the car."

"Me too," Penny said. "Cameras, maybe? It's creepy. And speaking of cameras, I bet Barry's really kicking himself for not keeping the ones at the museum in peak condition. Or not, if Lee is right." She related the archaeologist's theory about the missing Lady.

"A fraudulent mummy," Finn said. "Now I've heard everything."

"Seriously." Penny snorted. "Hopefully the Garda are checking stolen artwork channels."

"I can inquire with Scotland Yard and Interpol," Finn offered. "Though from what you've told me, it sounds more personal than a targeted art theft."

"I agree," Penny said. "People's identities and businesses are really wrapped up in the Lady here. And let me tell you what I learned about Muriel Gleason." She told Finn about Caroline's relationship to the storekeeper. "So there's a local connection and maybe a motive for murder."

"Who else do you have for suspects?" Finn asked. "Purely as a matter of intellectual inquiry."

Penny smiled. "I like the way you put that. Well, there's Oliver, her ex-husband and professional rival. Barry Danvers, the museum director, didn't want Caroline to have the Lady examined. His ancestor found the bog body, by the way. So he's a suspect."

"Refresh me. Why did Caroline want to examine the body?"

"I'm not sure. I think the threat is what she might have learned. Lee confirmed this theory for me."

"Something that discredits the accepted story?" Finn guessed.

"Yes. They can find out where a body is from by analyzing the hair. Lee thinks the bog body might not be from Ireland at all."

"Wow. If Caroline had discovered the body was a fraud, then the museum would lose all credibility."

"The other businesses would be hurt too," Penny said. "They use the Lady in their advertising and on all kinds of gift items they sell to tourists."

Finn gave a low whistle. "Plenty of motive there. Caroline isn't the only one who wanted to examine the Lady, however. Lee's on the trail too, you said. Plus, other researchers might be interested in the future."

"In the Lady who is now missing?" Penny pointed out.

"Yes, but if a local took her, they can't keep her hidden forever. Not without damaging the museum and other businesses too."

"You're right." Resting her chin on her drawn-up knees, Penny stared out at the water. "Everything is such a snarl right now."

"Something will eventually break," Finn said. "It always does." After a beat, he asked, "What about the other two archaeologists?

Lee and Paige? Any motives there regarding Caroline?"

"Nothing overt," Penny said. "Remember the eccentric woman I mentioned? Kinzi Eagan, the one who dresses like the Lady sometimes? She's definitely protective of her. She roams the island, claiming to be a direct descendant, though I'm not sure how she could know that."

"Could Kinzi be a suspect?" Finn asked. "If she thought Caroline was threatening her ancestor, she'd have a motive."

Penny pictured Kinzi confronting Caroline, then pushing her off the cliff. "She's certainly passionate enough, if older and not as fit as Caroline. Actually, I could be wrong about her fitness. She has a cleaning business."

"People can have amazing strength when they're in a rage," Finn said. "I wouldn't rule her out."

"Kinzi does cleaning work at the caravan park, so she has an excuse to be there," Penny admitted. "Her odd behavior doesn't necessarily make her a suspect, though."

"Agreed," Finn said. "That's lazy detective work. Although she has a motive if she's as obsessed with the bog body as you say."

Penny recalled how Kinzi had acted on the beach, as if she were role-playing her ancestor. Not many people went that far. "She's obsessed all right."

"In other news," Finn said. "I can't wait to finish training and come join you."

Penny's heart leaped. "Me neither. Maybe we can go fishing." Fishing was one of Finn's favorite outdoor activities, and he'd been teaching Penny.

"Sea kayaking too. Have you done that?"

"In San Diego, yes," Penny said. "Doing it in a different ocean will be a new adventure. The weather has been perfect so far."

Finn made a sound. "That might change tomorrow. There's the possibility of a severe storm. You won't want to be out on the water in that. Keep your eyes on the forecast."

"I will," Penny promised, hoping the storm wouldn't blow in while they were still camping out at the site. "Speaking of being on the water, I piloted the motorboat out to the island." She told him about that learning experience.

"Good job." Finn briefly pulled away from the phone. "Unfortunately, someone is calling me. Talk soon?"

"You bet," Penny said. "You'll get all the updates, good and bad."

"Hopefully mostly good. You've had quite a bit of excitement on this relaxing vacation of yours."

"All too true."

They signed off with words of affection. Penny sighed. She couldn't wait to see Finn. And Nan. And the cats. Not to mention her coworkers and customers at The Merry Teapot too. She was at the point on a trip when she was starting to get homesick, but she felt a rush of happiness when she realized she didn't miss California. Blarney Green had become her real home.

Penny made an easy dinner of sandwiches and soup. Penny, Nora, and Lee sat around the table, each lost in their own world. Nora worked on sketches for her map and Lee was deep in research. Penny read a book on her phone, glad to escape real life for a while.

Then her battery icon flashed red. "Uh-oh," she said. "How do we charge our phones?"

"Solar charger," Lee said, pointing to an orange-and-black device sitting on the table. "Should be ready to use."

Penny retrieved a cord from her bag. As she dug, she came across the binoculars Finn had given her. She'd forgotten all about them. Slinging the strap around her neck, she returned to the dining area and plugged in her phone. "So glad we have this charger," she said. "I wouldn't like to be out here with a dead phone. Any news from Oliver?"

"He texted me a while ago. They made it to Dublin okay." Lee was poring over a local map.

"Are you helping Nora with her map?" Penny asked.

"What? No, I'm checking out the lay of the land." Lee glanced at Nora. "What are you doing?"

"I'm creating a map of Beag Anoach with hand lettering and fanciful illustrations." Nora showed him the drawing pad. "I want to make them available for sale."

"Nice." Lee smiled. "I love that type of map."

"Me too," Penny agreed. "I'm sure it will be a huge success." The sun was sinking below the hills on the mainland. "I'm going to take Corky for a walk before bed."

"Thanks," Nora said, bending over her drawing pad again.

Although she wanted to keep charging her phone, she unhooked it from the battery and put it in her pocket, thinking she'd rather have it in case of an emergency. Penny called to Corky, who was lying near Nora's feet, and then the pair set off across the bluff. The tall grass waved in the evening breeze, and birds circled and called. The setting sun gilded the waves in the water below as they rippled endlessly toward shore.

This exact view has been the same for millennia, Penny reflected with awe. Countless women her age had probably stood right in the same spot enjoying the sunset over the centuries.

Shifting in the other direction, toward Anoach Island, she caught a glimpse of a red car zipping along the headland. Penny snatched the binoculars around her neck and pressed them to her eyes.

She saw a crumpled fender when she zoomed in, confirming it was the car she'd seen in the barn. She adjusted the lenses to examine the driver. He or she wore a hat and a pair of sunglasses. After another few moments, the car went around a curve, out of view.

Penny was disappointed that she hadn't identified the driver, but at least she had confirmed that the car was still on Anoach Island.

Pulling out her cell phone, she sent Detective Inspector Babcock a text.

On Beag Anoach. Just saw the red car on the headland opposite, crumpled fender and all. Couldn't identify driver.

Her duty done, Penny put away her phone, eager to stretch her legs before bed. "Race you to that rock, Corky," she called. They dashed across the grass, Penny laughing and Corky yipping in excitement.

After a few more minutes, they circled around to the campsite, where Penny plugged her phone back into the charger for a boost while she boiled water for cocoa. The trio enjoyed the hot drink with a snack, then headed for bed.

Penny unzipped the tent and crawled inside, her knees feeling the bumpy earth through the thin pad beneath her sleeping bag. "I'm so tired that even the ground feels comfortable."

"Me too," Nora said. She patted the tent floor at her feet. "Lie down, Corky." He slept inside with them.

"I saw the red car on Anoach," Penny told Nora as she lifted the binoculars strap over her head. She hadn't wanted to bring up the sighting in front of Lee and have to explain the whole story. "Unfortunately, I couldn't see the driver's face. I sent Babcock a text. No answer yet."

"She's probably busy," Nora said. "I hope it's with keeping an eye on this place. We don't need any uninvited visitors tonight."

"Or any other time," Penny said. As she shifted on the hard ground, she found herself hoping they'd return to the caravan soon in spite of her words to Nora. In comparison to a sleeping bag on the ground, the little bunk bed in the caravan was luxurious. "Good night, Nora."

"Good night, Penny. Sleep tight."

Penny was dreaming about dogs. Fluffy, friendly, barking dogs—then the noise finally penetrated. *Corky.*

She was in a tent on Beag Anoach, and Corky was barking.

She sat up. "Nora," she whispered. "What's going on?"

"Hush." Nora tugged at Corky's collar to move him aside so she could unzip the tent. "Someone is out there."

Penny joined her at the tent flap. A light floated around the dig site. They had company.

15

"Maybe it's Lee," Penny suggested, although surely he would wait for daylight to poke around. Then a second light appeared and smashed that theory.

"Come on," Nora said. "We need to check it out." She crawled through the opening.

"What about Corky?" Penny asked. She had to use her body to block him from pushing outside in pursuit of his owner.

Nora had her phone, and she shined its flashlight into the tent. "Grab his leash. We'll bring him, just in case."

Penny found the leash and clipped it on his collar, then handed it to Nora so Corky could go out first. Otherwise she risked being run over by an anxious dog. She also grabbed her flashlight and phone.

"We need backup," Penny said, detouring toward Lee's tent. She hunkered down near the tent entrance. "Lee? Lee. We have visitors."

No response. Maybe he was a deep sleeper. She bent closer to listen. Not even a snore or rustle of a sleeping bag.

"I don't think he's in there," Penny told Nora.

"Take a peek," Nora suggested.

Penny was hesitant to intrude in case she was wrong. Finally, she unzipped the front flap a couple of inches. "Lee? Are you in there?" she said through the gap.

Again, there was no answer.

She dared to pull the zipper down further. Switching on her flashlight, she aimed the beam inside. The tent was empty, the sleeping bag lying flat.

"He isn't here."

Nora glanced toward the dig site. "Maybe he's out there."

"I don't want to assume that." Penny was uneasy about confronting whoever it was. "They might be dangerous."

"True." Nora put a hand to her chin, thinking. "I don't want to call the Garda yet, in case it *is* him. They wouldn't be happy."

"Can we sneak over?" Penny asked. There wasn't much foliage around the site. "Maybe we can go up the hill and circle around to a spot where we can listen. We'll recognize Lee's voice."

Nora studied the landscape. "All right. We'll try it. Corky, you need to be quiet." He answered with a little whine as though reluctantly assenting.

They crept along, doing their best to be quiet. Once Penny's eyes adjusted, she could see any obstacles fairly well, not that there were many. Once they reached the vantage point, they sat, not wanting to be spotted as darker figures against the sky.

The first clear sound was the strike of a shovel against a rock, followed by a grunt. Someone was digging.

"Maybe you found the treasure," a man called in a low voice.

One of the lights dipped closer to the ground, and the digger made a sound of disgust. "It's a rock."

"Is that Carroll?" Penny whispered in Nora's ear.

"I think so." Nora began tapping her phone screen. "I'm calling the Garda."

While her cousin made the call, Penny studied the dig site. There was no sign of Lee. Where could he be? Her heart thumped as a terrible thought struck.

"They're on their way," Nora said.

Penny grabbed her cousin's arm. "What if they hurt Lee? Maybe he confronted them." She imagined Lee lying on the ground, injured. Or worse.

Nora gasped. "I hope not."

"How long did the dispatcher say it would be?"

"Fifteen minutes. They need to come over from the harbor on Anoach Island."

That felt like a lifetime. Penny scanned the dig site for any sign of Lee. If only she dared to shine a light on the area to really check for him. Corky would defend them if they were confronted, but she didn't want to take the risk of the dog getting hurt either.

"I don't know what to do," Penny said with a groan. "Lee might need our help."

Nora rose to her feet. "We can check the path to the dock. Maybe he heard their boat and went to see who was coming."

They trekked along the rise to where the path went down to the cove. No one was on the trail, beside it, or down by the water.

Penny shined her flashlight on the boats tied to the dock. Instead of Carroll's usual craft, a shiny new motorboat bobbed on a line. "Nice boat."

"Quite an upgrade," Nora agreed. "Our boat is still here, so Lee didn't leave the island unless someone picked him up."

"I'm calling him." Penny wasn't sure why she hadn't tried that earlier. She found Lee's name in her list of contacts and dialed. "No answer," she said a moment later. "It rang and rang."

"Well, it is the middle of the night," Nora noted. "But if he went somewhere, he should have told us."

"I can't believe he would leave the dig unattended and put his job at risk," Penny protested. Surely he didn't expect her and Nora to act as the lone guards. They weren't even official members of the team.

"Did you think he'd lie about anything else the way he lied about being sick?" Nora asked. "That showed me that he's more interested in his own advancement than the dig."

"True," Penny admitted. Was it a case of Lee being his unreliable self? She would rather have that be true than a more nefarious alternative.

The grumble of a powerful boat engine cut through the night, indicating the Garda were on their way. Penny and Nora waited on the shore as the large craft approached.

Footsteps pounded on the path, and two figures came down the hill, lights swinging. "I was right," one said. "It's the Garda."

"Keep moving," the other said. Definitely Carroll.

Penny shined her light on the men, who ducked. Both held shovels and wore headlamps and backpacks. With the Garda in view, she was confident they wouldn't do anything to hurt her and Nora. "What did you do with Lee?" she demanded.

"Lee?" Carroll skidded to a stop. "Haven't seen him."

"Well, he's missing, and he was here earlier," Penny said. "Before you showed up."

Carroll lurched into movement. "Nothing to do with us." His friend was already on the dock, untying the lines securing the boat.

"Nice boat," Penny called. "New?"

In response, the two men leaped aboard and started the engine, backed away from the dock, and headed out into the water. Away from the Garda, Penny noticed.

"That was brave of you," Nora said.

"Not really. They weren't going to do much with the Garda upon us."

The Garda's boat engine throttled down as it approached the dock. A large searchlight mounted on the front swept the shore, picking out Penny and Nora, who winced in the glare and waved.

"All right out here?" a man called.

"We had intruders, but they took off," Nora said. "Carroll Gleason was one of them."

"How many were there?" he asked.

"Two," Nora answered. "The other was male also. We didn't recognize him. Well, I didn't. Did you, Penny?"

"No," Penny said. "He was a stranger. By the way, Carroll has a new boat." She relayed the few details she remembered.

"Do you want us to take you to Anoach?" the garda asked. "We're quite happy to."

"If we leave, Carroll and his pal will probably be right back," Nora said to Penny.

"Plus, we need to search for Lee," Penny said. She shifted and called to the garda, "We have a missing person. Lee Cameron, one of the archaeologists." She pointed to the small boat tied at the dock. "The boat we use is still here. He's not in his tent or at the dig site." With Carroll's denial, which had sounded sincere, she wasn't as concerned that he'd been attacked. He might be hurt, though.

"Hold on." The garda conferred with another officer, then returned. "We're going to come ashore."

The craft nudged closer, and the officers secured it at the dock. Two male gardaí—one very tall, the other short and stocky—soon joined them on shore, both holding powerful flashlights. The tall one identified himself as Garda Franklin, while the shorter man was Garda Griffin. Nora introduced herself, Penny, and Corky, then they led the way up the hill. In the glow of their flashlights, Penny recognized them as having been on the island during the gold coin handover.

"So you got treasure hunters already," Garda Franklin said as they went up the rise. "Not a surprise, really. Your find was incredible."

"Put this place squarely on the map, it did," Garda Griffin said. "You might need to get better security out here." He shook his head. "Two women and a dog. No offense, but not quite adequate to protect such an important site."

"We had Lee too," Penny said. "I agree with you, though. Especially after tonight."

"Those were locals," Griffin said. "You might get people from all over out here digging up the place." He gave a laugh. "Might post a sign in my garden next spring. 'Treasure here.' Get those lads to turn over the soil for me."

The joke lightened the atmosphere, which Penny appreciated. Since long-term security at the site wasn't feasible, she hoped Oliver and his team could thoroughly explore the main village area in one season. After that, if people wanted to dig up the whole island, more power to them. At least they wouldn't be interfering with a valuable archaeological site.

As they came over the rise and headed down toward the dig, the gardaí shined their spotlights over the area. Penny groaned. Even at a glance, she could tell that Carroll and his friend had damaged an area adjacent to a trench. Heaps of soil revealed how carelessly and quickly they'd dug into the earth.

"That spot's no good now," Nora said glumly. "Who knows what they ruined?"

Even if they sifted all the soil and found artifacts, the layering information was gone. Proving their age would be more difficult.

Leaving an examination of the dig for later, they showed the officers Lee's tent. "He was still up when we went to bed," Nora said. "He didn't say anything about leaving the island to me. Did he mention anything to you, Penny?"

Penny shook her head. "Not a peep. He knew how important it was to be here so we could stop people from digging. Not that we succeeded," she added. Maybe they should have taken shifts, the way they had when the gold was discovered.

Garda Griffin aimed his light inside Lee's tent. "Nothing of interest here. His computer is still there." He backed out and stood.

"Did you call him?"

"Yes, but no answer," Penny said. "Want his number?"

"Sure." Garda Franklin entered the digits into his own phone. "Right to voice mail." He left a message saying for Lee to get in touch with the garda or Nora and Penny. After he hung up, he said, "We'll take a walk around, see if we can find him."

Since the area was a few acres in size, they split up, Nora with Franklin, Penny with Griffin. After a few questions about Penny, such as where she was from and what she was doing on the dig, they lapsed into silence as they methodically searched the dig area and the grasslands surrounding it.

"There's no sign of him or any other boats," Garda Franklin said as they met up. "I can't think what else to do until morning when we can search in daylight."

"Could be he'll show up by then," Griffin said. "We don't have any signs of foul play or misadventure."

Penny knew they were right. Lee wasn't exactly reliable from what she'd seen so far. They could spend all night searching the island in the dark, then have him appear chipper and wondering what the fuss was all about in the morning.

Garda Franklin gave them his number. "Call if there is any sign of trouble at all. We'll be swinging past here regularly."

"Thank you," Nora said. "Hopefully we'll spend the rest of the night in peace."

Penny offered tea, which the gardaí declined with thanks and then left.

"I'm putting the kettle on," Penny said. "I'll never get back to sleep now."

Nora sighed. "Me neither. My brain is whirring."

In the dining area, Penny switched on the hanging lantern and started the kettle while Nora gave Corky a snack.

"You're a good boy," Nora told him. "Our living alarm system."

"I was dreaming about barking dogs," Penny said. "Then I woke up and realized it was real."

"Very real." Seated at the table, Nora rested her chin on her hand. "That was a shady thing for Carroll to do. Surely he knows better."

"I wonder what else he's up to," Penny said. "He got the money for that new boat somewhere." Had Carroll found artifacts and sold them? The kettle whistled, so she made two cups of tea and took them to the table.

"Maybe he saved up," Nora said. "You're right, though. It's worth questioning."

"I'll mention him to Finn." Penny blew on her tea. "He was going to check with Scotland Yard and Interpol about the Lady. They have officers who track stolen antiquities. If Carroll or anyone else is illicitly selling Iron Age artifacts, they'll probably know."

"Great idea." Nora picked up her mug. "How's Finn doing?"

"I think he's enjoying his training. When he comes here at the end of my stay, he wants to do some fishing and sea kayaking."

"I'd like to as well," Nora said. "I've had more than enough of crime investigations."

"Seriously." Penny reviewed the situation. "Hit-and-run. Murder. Theft. A missing colleague. Now vandalism, I guess you'd call it."

"Destruction of a protected site?" Nora suggested. "Not sure if it's listed as one."

A pang of worry concerning Lee hit Penny. Where was he? If he'd gone for a walk and fallen asleep somewhere or left the island without telling them, she'd be furious.

"I hope Oliver figures out better security," Nora said. "Now that they've found gold, I bet the dig goes on for a couple of years at least."

"The treasure will definitely pique curiosity all over. Speaking of which, how is your map coming?" If Penny wanted to get any sleep, she had to slow down her brain. Her thoughts were going around and around in circles with no off-ramp. *Who hit Kenneth? Who killed Caroline? Where is the Lady? And what about Lee?*

"I'll show you." Nora had left her sketch pad on the table, so she grabbed it and flipped it open to a two-page spread. "This is a rough draft," she warned.

Penny, who was used to Nora's unnecessary disclaimers, smiled as she took in the drawing. It depicted Beag Anoach, with little emblems marking information and points of interest. The headland where they worked was marked by conical Iron Age houses. Sea creatures swam around the island, and seabirds flew overhead. On the highest point stood the Lady, her cloak whipped by the wind.

"It's beautiful and whimsical, but also useful," Penny said. "I love it."

Nora smiled with pride. "Thanks. I'm really having fun. I figure I can always release additional versions as Oliver's team learns more."

They studied the map together as they sipped tea. Gradually, a pleasant exhaustion began to creep over Penny. "I think I can sleep now."

"Me too." Nora finished her tea. "Let's stay in bed tomorrow. We don't have any reason to get up, do we?"

"Not until we're hungry," Penny said. She didn't have to cook breakfast for a crowd, which meant she could laze around. She tidied up their cups and followed Nora and Corky to the tent. She hoped her sleep wouldn't be interrupted again by yet another crisis. She'd endured plenty for one week.

Penny's desire was granted. It was almost nine in the morning when she awoke. Nora was still curled up in her sleeping bag. Corky caught Penny's eye and whined.

"You poor thing," she cooed to the patient dog. "You want to go out, don't you?"

Since Penny was already wearing a T-shirt and flannel pajama pants, she threw on a jacket and slid her feet into clogs. One advantage of being in the middle of nowhere was that their sole company was Lee.

Lee. Penny's urgency to leave the tent ramped up. She needed to see if he'd returned. She let the dog out, then slid through the opening after him. Heart in her throat, she crossed the dewy grass to Lee's tent.

Once again, she bent close and called, "Lee? Are you in there?"

Again, silence met her ears.

"I'm going to unzip your tent," Penny warned, giving him a chance to protest. When none came, she pulled the zipper down enough so she could peek inside.

The tent was empty.

In the glow of sunlight, she spotted something else. A wallet lay partially tucked under his pillow. She could understand him leaving his computer, which was still there among his other belongings. His wallet shouldn't be, not if he'd left the island.

Something was definitely wrong.

16

Penny peered around Lee's tent, hoping he might have left a note about his whereabouts, so that she at least had a direction to search. Not that he seemed the type. She was being thorough.

"It's a mystery, Corky," she told the dog as she backed out of Lee's tent. Rather than wake Nora, she went to the dining area to feed Corky and put the kettle on, two constants in an uncertain world.

While Corky ate, Penny sat at the table to wait on the kettle. The morning sun made dew droplets shine in the grass. Seabirds swooped and cried over the water while songbirds greeted the beautiful day as they flitted about the scattered trees.

Where could Lee be? Had he gone for a walk around the island? She and Nora should make a circuit later. If he had gone out on his own or left the island, he was in for the scolding of his life. It wasn't fair of him to put them through so much worry, not to mention making them responsible for the dig.

Rising from her chair, she scanned the trench area. It was the same as last night, with Carroll's reckless digging marring the end of one section near where the gold was found, which she supposed was a logical place to hunt for more treasure.

The kettle began to hum. Rather than let it whistle, Penny switched off the heat. She'd bring Nora tea in bed, returning the favor from the other morning.

Corky on her heels, Penny carried the two mugs to the tent.

She set the mugs down carefully and unzipped the flap, then crawled in, retrieved the tea, and said, "Good morning."

Nora shifted with a slight groan. Pushing her hair back from her face, she sat up. "You brought me tea?" She accepted the mug. "Lovely."

Penny let her drink a few swallows before saying, "Lee is still gone. And guess what? I saw his wallet in the tent."

The implications quickly sank in. "He wouldn't leave his wallet if he went off the island."

"I agree. We should take a lap around the whole island and see if he's hurt somewhere."

"Makes sense." Nora sipped tea. "How does the dig look in daylight?"

"They were digging near where I found the gold," Penny said. "If they disturbed anywhere else, I didn't see it."

"I guess we heard them in time," Nora said. "After we search for Lee, we can sift the soil they dug up and pull out any artifacts even though we won't have position data for them."

"That'll be a good way to pass the time until Oliver returns." Penny winced. "He is going to be pretty upset."

"That's probably an understatement." Nora glanced at her phone. "I need to charge this, then I'll try to reach him. He should hear the updates as soon as we can provide them."

After they drank the tea, Penny left the tent to start breakfast while Nora got dressed. She decided on fried eggs. As she worked, she noticed a line of clouds to the southwest. Was rain on the way, as Finn had warned her? She hoped not.

Nora emerged, and they sat down to their meal. After they cleaned up, Nora tried to call Oliver but got his voice mail. Next, they went to assess the damage wrought by Carroll and his friend. The two men had created a crater in the ground, with a heap of dirt that reached Penny's waist.

"Ugh," Penny said. "They really did wreck this area."

"The good news is that I don't think they found anything," Nora said. "But still, how could someone have so little regard for history?"

"I'm glad we were here. And that Corky woke us up." Penny pictured the entire site littered with holes. She took out her phone and snapped a few photos.

"What are you doing?" Nora asked.

"Oliver might want to press charges. When we sift the soil, we'll destroy the evidence of what they did." Penny stood back to get a wide shot.

"Smart thinking." Nora gave the area a final scan. "Let's get the map and take our walk."

"We should pack water and snacks. Who knows how long it will take?" Penny also made a mental note to grab her binoculars.

"We can grab treats and a bowl for Corky too," Nora said.

The official map showed terrain lines and elevation, which was useful. Their first stop was the height of land, where they could view much of the island. From there, the dig was laid out before their eyes, former settlements shaping the landscape under the grass.

In the other direction lay Anoach Island. "That's where I saw the red car." Penny pointed to the road along the headland. "Unfortunately, I didn't get a good view of the driver."

"That's too bad," Nora said. "I hope the Garda catch up with the driver soon."

"Me too." Penny spotted the trail that led over to the other side. "Why don't we take that path and see where it leads? We already checked for Lee at the boat landing."

They stood facing the mainland, so the boat landing was located to their left. The new trail went to the right, toward a side of the island they hadn't searched yet.

"Sure, why not?" Nora started toward the path. "Exploring is fun. I wish we were doing it under other circumstances."

"So do I."

The new trail led along a bluff before beginning a gradual descent toward the shore. At one point, they entered an enchanting copse of trees twisted by the incessant sea wind. If they hadn't been searching for a missing man, Penny would enjoy the explorations as much as Nora seemed to.

Nora halted in the middle of the grove. "I would love to paint this place. It's beautiful." She took a couple of photos with her phone.

"I hope you do," Penny said. "Corky and I can hold down the fort."

"We'll see." Nora exhaled. "Right now, all I can focus on is Lee." As she started to put her phone away, it rang. She checked the screen. "It's Oliver." She answered, then pulled the phone away and pressed another command. "I'm putting you on speaker."

"Okay." Oliver's voice rang out clearly. "What's going on? Your message said it was urgent."

"Last night, Carroll Gleason and his friend started digging up an area near a trench," Nora reported, and Oliver exclaimed in shock and anger. "I called the Garda, who came out pretty quickly. Carroll and his friend ran away, but we got a good look at them and their boat. Carroll has a new one."

"Interesting," Oliver said. "So is there anything you need me to do?"

"Not until you get back. You could press charges. They interfered with a section of the dig." Nora paused for breath. "One more thing. Lee is gone."

It took Oliver a moment to respond. "What do you mean, gone?"

"As in nowhere to be found on the island. The boat is here, and so is his tent."

"And his wallet and computer," Penny put in.

"That's strange." Oliver's tone sharpened. "Is he lying hurt somewhere? I sure hope not."

"We wondered that as well," Nora said. "We're going over the island right now searching for him."

Penny wondered if she should tell Oliver about Lee's previous unreliability. She normally didn't like to snitch on people, but Lee's behavior was becoming a pattern. "Oliver, there's something you need to hear."

"Go ahead, Penny." Trepidation was heavy in his voice.

"Remember when Lee was sick and didn't go out to the dig?" Penny asked.

"I do."

"Well, he wasn't sick. He was faking it. I saw him in town, and he confessed."

"What? Why on earth would he do that?" Oliver sounded both hurt and angry.

Penny decided not to betray Lee's confidence about his secret project. It didn't really matter to Oliver what exactly he was doing, only that Lee had let the team down.

"He's working on a project for himself," she said. "I'll leave it to him to tell you about it."

"All right. I'm going to have a little talk with Lee when I get back, then. Please don't tell him that, okay?"

"We won't," Penny said. "It's really not our business."

"As of now, I won't be back until tomorrow," Oliver said. "I've got more meetings and such. You should be seeing Paige anytime, though. She left this morning."

"Great," Penny said, glad that they'd have another crew member on-site.

"Keep an eye on the weather, okay?" Oliver warned. "I also heard that a storm might be coming in."

Nora rolled her eyes. "That's all we need. Thanks for the heads-up."

"You might want to head back to the caravan park. I hate to think of you trying to brave rough weather at the site," Oliver said. "Either way, keep in touch. I'm worried about you two. I never should have left."

"We'll be fine," Nora assured him. "I'll check in later."

Nora put away her phone, and they continued along the path. Penny found herself casting glances toward the bank of clouds in the distance. She hoped that the storm would fizzle out or take a different path. Sleeping in a tent during a rainstorm would not be fun.

After leaving the woods, the trail continued to descend in switchbacks. The gradient was gentle and the views spectacular. The last section was a rutted, narrow path between big, blocky boulders that led to a small beach embraced by rocks that jutted into the water.

"A boat could land here," Nora said, going to the edge of the water. "It's sandy quite a distance out."

Penny wondered if the beach was ever used for that purpose. "We'll have to mention it to Oliver if they decide to add security to the dig site."

"Good idea." Nora walked back and forth across the small beach, pebbles and sand crunching under her sneakers. She stared up at the bluff. "Oliver's Beag Anoach history book mentioned a smuggler's cave. I wonder if it's up there."

Penny felt a surge of excitement. The Irish and British coasts had been known for smuggling exploits hundreds of years ago. One famous spot near Blarney Green was Dutchman's Cove. "Were they pirates?"

"Maybe." Nora smiled. "Inspiration for map emblems, anyway."

The trail picked up again at the end of the beach, rising across the headland. The path skirted the edge of the land, giving a view of the rocks below. Heart in her throat, Penny stopped every few steps and scanned the rocks to make sure that Lee hadn't fallen.

"Still no sign of him," Penny said as the path led them away from the shore. "He must have left the island."

"It sure seems that way." Nora stopped to rest. "Maybe try calling him again?"

Penny tried, but the call went immediately to voice mail. "Either he doesn't want to hear from me, or his phone is off or out of power."

Nora huffed a breath. "We've given it our best shot. If he doesn't want to be found, what can we do? At least he isn't injured somewhere on the island. Not that we've found anyway."

Penny was somewhat cheered by Nora's summation, though she'd feel much better once Lee showed up or got back in touch. Her belly rumbled, turning her thoughts to something more pleasant. "Let's go have lunch. I'm starving."

Back at the site, Penny made peanut butter sandwiches and heated soup. They were eating when the first strong gust of wind swept through.

"Here it comes," Nora said, studying the sky.

The cloud cover had crept in faster than Penny would have thought possible. In the bay, the waves thundered, tossing spray as they crashed against the shore.

"I think we should leave the island," Nora said. "Now."

They raced through the rest of their meal, then packed their clothing and other belongings as the tent was buffeted by the wind. Penny didn't bother with food. They had plenty back at the caravan.

Anxiety began to gnaw at Penny. Piloting the small boat was easy enough when it was calm. Would they make it safely to the other side in rough conditions?

"What should we do about the others' belongings?" Penny asked as a new worry struck. If the tents leaked, the contents could be ruined. "Especially Lee's laptop."

"Grab it," Nora said. "He'll probably appreciate it."

Penny dashed over to Lee's tent. Inside, she found the laptop sleeve and slid the device inside. She also took his wallet so it wouldn't get soaked. A small spiral-bound notebook with a pretty cover caught her eye. Thinking it was an odd item for Lee to own, she flipped it open.

Caroline's name was written inside. Penny leafed through a few pages of handwritten notes. Why did Lee have it? Did it mean he had killed Caroline?

A phrase jumped out at her from the page. *The Lady*. Lee must have taken the notebook to learn Caroline's thoughts about the bog body.

After a moment's hesitation, Penny took the notebook as well. When they finally tracked Lee down, they'd ask him about it.

Then she ran back to join Nora, who was waiting near their tent. Rain began to fall in slanting sheets. Penny stuffed Lee's belongings and the notebook deep into her duffel, where they would be safe from getting wet. They both donned rain slickers, Nora's pink and Penny's green.

Nora whistled for Corky, and they set off on the trail, almost trotting up the rise. Penny panted for breath, burdened as she was by her duffel and sleeping bag. An urgency to get across the bay kept her going.

As they started down the other side, Nora gave a shout. Penny had been watching her feet so she wouldn't trip and fall. At first, she didn't notice anything wrong. Nora was still upright and the dog was staying close to their heels.

Then she saw the empty dock.

The small boat was gone. They had no way to get off the island.

17

"You've got to be kidding," Nora said through gritted teeth. "The boat is gone?"

"I thought I tied it tightly enough," Penny said miserably. "Lee helped me." She distinctly remembered him cleating the line.

"Then I'm sure it was fine. Someone probably took it."

A chill ran through Penny. "You mean someone was on the island?" Had it been Lee? Or a stranger?

"I sure hope it was Lee," Nora said emphatically. She whirled around on the trail. "Back we go. Hurry, before we're soaked."

They trudged back up the hill toward the dig site. Storm or not, they'd probably have to spend the night on the island. "Do you think the Garda would come rescue us?" Penny asked.

"Maybe," Nora said. They stopped again and gazed at the bay, where waves lunged toward shore, crashing on impact. "The conditions are getting pretty bad."

Penny thought she might try calling the Garda once they reached the campsite. If they had to stay, they were in for a long and miserable night. Her brothers, Connor and Peter, relished outdoor adventures and would probably see it as a challenge. Maybe she should try to frame it that way for herself.

After dropping off her belongings, Penny left Nora tightening the rain fly and the tent pegs while she went to forage dinner. She needed to put something together that they could eat in their tent since the open-sided canopy was too exposed to be pleasant.

Penny found some freeze-dried meals. All she had to do was add hot water and let them sit for a few minutes. She returned to the tent. Corky and Nora were both seated under the extended portion of the fly, watching the rain.

"I've got dinner sorted," Penny said. "Instant meals. We can make them when the rain lets up a little."

"A warm meal actually sounds pretty good," Nora said.

"It'll be easy too. Is there room for me?" Penny squeezed in beside Nora and sat cross-legged on the ground. Unzipping her pocket, she found her phone. "Let's call the Garda."

She scrolled through and located Garda Franklin's number. After a few rings, he answered. Penny identified herself, and he immediately asked if the intruders had come back.

"Not that we've seen," she answered. "But we have a bit of a situation. Our boat is missing, and we're stranded here on Beag Anoach."

"Do you have shelter?" he asked. "Food and water?" When she answered in the affirmative, he said, "You'll have to stay put for the time being. A small craft advisory has been posted, and we're handling several emergencies right now."

"I understand." Penny was glad that at least they were on firm ground rather than floundering in the cold sea. "We'll hunker down for the night, I guess."

"Once the storm passes, someone will come get you," the garda said. "I'll make a note that you're stranded, okay?"

"Thank you. We appreciate your help." After a few more pleasantries, Penny disconnected the call.

"They're not coming, are they?" Nora asked, her voice resigned.

"We'll have to make the best of it." Ruffling her dog's ears, she added, "Right, Corky?" He leaned into her hand with a happy groan, and they laughed.

Penny and Nora watched the rain for a while before retreating to the inside of the tent. "Let me know when you're hungry, and I'll run out and make our dinner." She grinned. "Such as it is." Rooting around in her duffel for fresh socks, she came across the notebook sitting on top of Lee's computer and withdrew it. "Check out what I found earlier."

Nora took the notebook, regarding it curiously. "In Lee's tent?"

"Yes. I also rescued his wallet in case the tent blew away or something."

Nora grimaced at that thought, then opened the notebook. "This belongs to Caroline."

Penny pulled out a folded pair of socks. "I wonder if Oliver has any idea Lee has it."

Their gazes met, and they chorused, "No way."

"So sneaky of Lee," Penny said. "I don't blame Oliver if he fires him. For all we know, the notebook has clues to Caroline's death."

Nora's eyes went wide. "You might be right." Her expression sobered. "That could be why he has it."

"I never thought of Lee as a suspect," Penny admitted. "I didn't think he had a motive."

"I didn't either," Nora said. "That's why it's important to keep an open mind, right?" She peered outside. "Should we eat soon? Then we can take our time going through the notebook."

"Sure." Penny reached for her slicker. "Two fake dinners coming right up."

"You make the meal sound so enticing," Nora said with a laugh. "I'll come with you. I need to feed Corky."

The pair slid on their raincoats and dashed with Corky to the dining canopy, which was flapping in the wind. Penny managed to get the camping stove going to boil water. Nora fed Corky, who shook and sent water droplets flying in every direction.

"This is going to be a night to remember," Penny said. "And not in a good way." Her fingers were red with cold, and rain slapped her in the face every few seconds.

"Think of the stories you'll tell. Meanwhile, grin and bear it." Nora demonstrated with a bare-toothed smile.

Penny laughed, shaking her head. "That was scary. Please don't make that face again."

Nora laughed too. "Think of the people who used to live here. They worked hard for everything they had, and they weathered worse storms than this. We're soft in comparison."

"True." The kettle whistled, and Penny added the water to their dinners and to a thermos for tea. "Can you fill a couple of water bottles? And grab some biscuits for dessert. Whatever we can take along to minimize our trips over here."

Heads bent against the wind, they made the trek back, reaching the barely adequate shelter of the tent with relief. At least it was dry and soon warm from the three of them crowded inside.

Penny put on a thick wool sweater, which helped, then dug into her meal. "This wasn't too bad," she said, spooning up the last bite of reconstituted chicken and rice.

"Hot and filling," Nora said, scraping her bowl clean. "Can't ask for much more than that in these conditions."

They put their dishes aside to wash later and lay down on the sleeping bags, the notebook and the tin of cookies between them. Corky lay across their feet, providing extra comfort.

"I'm so glad we brought him," Penny said. "He's been a real help." She thought of how he'd warned them about intruders more than once, which led to a thought. "I wonder if Carroll tried to break into Kenneth's caravan that first night. He's certainly hot on the trail of antiquities."

"I considered that too," Nora said. "He's been around enough to know that important finds were stored in there." She tapped her finger on the notebook. "Ready to read?"

"Definitely." Penny moved a couple of inches closer.

The first entries in Caroline's notebook were dated in June. Penny gathered that she used the notebook to record thoughts about projects of interest. The first mention of Beag Anoach appeared partway through the month.

> *Spoke to Kenneth about joining the Beag Anoach dig. It's interesting enough that I wouldn't mind a junior role. He told me there wasn't enough funding, but I could volunteer. No thanks. I did that when I was an undergrad.*

A few pages later, she wrote:

> *Reconsidering Kenneth's offer. I'm free this summer, and it might be time to do something about the so-called Lady. After my trip to Denmark, I started wondering if she really is Irish. Lee Cameron might be on to something. He tried to be cagey, but I knew what he was hinting at. Wouldn't it be fun to scoop him? After all, I have more connection to Anoach than he ever will. It's my turf.*

"Wow," Penny said. "I wonder if Lee knew what she was thinking."

"If he did, then he had a motive to argue with her, maybe even kill her," Nora mused.

"That seems extreme."

"Normally, but we're discussing academics. Everything is life or death to them. In this case, whoever got there first with the Lady would get a real career boost. Television appearances, maybe even a documentary, conferences, papers, a book. Scandals and controversy are catnip in that arena."

"In every arena," Penny noted sadly. She'd lived through a similar situation herself when a mismatch went viral.

Nora patted her arm, obviously guessing what she was thinking. "It all worked out. Now you're here with me."

"On an island in a tent during a rainstorm?" Penny raised a brow. "How lovely."

"You know what I mean." Nora turned back to the notebook.

Big news. Poor Kenneth is in the hospital. I worked my magic with the department head, and now the assignment is mine. Oliver won't be happy, but he'll have to deal. My plan this summer is to get samples from the Lady and have them analyzed. That will prove that she's not from Ireland. If we're really lucky, we'll find a connection to her original location. I'm sure it's near where Professor Danvers first visited. The truth might be delayed, obscured, even denied, but it always comes out.

Penny raised an eyebrow and pointed at the last line. "You could say that about murder too."

Once they'd gleaned all they could from Caroline's notebook, the cousins played backgammon on a portable game board. Meanwhile, the wind howled and the rain lashed. With every gust, Penny prayed that the tent would hold. If it leaked or was blown down, they would have to run to another tent. And if that collapsed too, they would really be in trouble.

"I suppose we should try to get some sleep," Nora said after losing the latest round of backgammon. "I'm losing my concentration."

Penny checked the weather on her phone. "The storm should move on sometime tonight, according to the radar map." The animation showed the clouds edging away.

"That's a relief." Nora put away her game and crawled into her sleeping bag. "We'll be able to go back to the caravan park." She gave a dramatic sigh. "I'm willing to swim, if need be. I can't wait to take a shower."

"Same." Penny slid into her own sleeping bag and tucked her phone under her pillow. Then she realized she hadn't conversed with Finn that evening and sat up again. "I'd better text Finn."

We got stuck in a storm on the small island, she texted him. *We're safe in our tent.*

You can't leave?

Rather than worry him with the missing boat, Penny wrote, *Small craft advisories. Storm should be over by dawn.*

Great. Can't wait to see you.

Ditto. Penny paused, wondering how much she should share. Then she went ahead and told him everything. *We found Caroline's notebook. She wanted to test the bog body because she thought it came from somewhere else. Lee has the same theory. We think it's a motive.*

For Lee? You haven't mentioned this to him, I hope.

Nope. He's missing. We wouldn't say anything anyway.

Missing? Penny could practically hear Finn's anxiety ratcheting up.

He disappeared last night. We have no idea where he is, although we searched the island for him in case he was hurt.

I don't like the sound of that.

Me neither, but we can't do anything about it tonight. And one more thing. Caroline's notebook was in Lee's tent. Whether he'd obtained it before or after her death was beside the point. He should have given it to the Garda.

I'm going to pass along this information, okay? I'll give the local Garda a heads-up.

Thanks. I could call, but they'd never hear me over the wind.

Hunker down. And please keep me posted.

I will. XO.

Penny lay down again and tucked the phone under her pillow.

"Anything to report?" Nora asked.

"He's going to contact the local Garda for us and tell them about the notebook. Lee should have handed it in."

"No kidding," Nora said.

"Of course, stealing a notebook pales compared to murder."

"True. On that pleasant thought, good night."

Penny fell into a doze, dimly aware of the rain and wind battering the tent. The sounds wove their way into her dreams, which featured torturous explorations of the island as she and Nora sought a way off to safety.

Silence and the glow of dawn woke her. The rain had stopped.

Corky whined softly, and Penny sat up. "You need to go out?"

Nora was still huddled in her sleeping bag. Penny pushed her feet into her sneakers, grabbed her binoculars, and crawled to the flap. Corky waited until the zipper rose enough to let him through, then bolted.

Penny followed more slowly, working to maintain her footing on the soggy ground. Pink and orange clouds drifted in a sky quickly becoming blue. The storm was over.

Corky cavorted about the grass, nose down whenever he caught an enticing odor. Penny crossed to the bluff to view the water, which was still turbulent but not as choppy as it had been during the storm. The wind was calmer as well, with an occasional gust. Her spirits rose. They would be able to leave the island soon.

Penny called Corky, who was wandering too far. The dog came running at a full gallop, tongue lolling, a sight that made her laugh.

As the pair started back toward the tent, a flash of yellow in the distance caught Penny's eye. What was that? Better yet, who was it? Had someone arrived on the island that morning?

Or had they been there all along?

18

Remembering her binoculars, Penny lifted them to her eyes. As the figure came into focus, Penny confirmed that it was a person wearing a rain slicker with the hood up. While she watched, they hurried away, back facing her so she couldn't see their features.

They must have spotted her in the open area, so why did they run away? Had they been hoping that the campsite was unattended and her presence had deterred them?

Was it Lee? If so, then his behavior was becoming stranger by the moment. Or was it someone scouting out the dig, hoping to unearth some treasures?

Penny ran back to the tent, eager to tell Nora about this latest development. "Nora," she said, crawling into the tent. "There's someone else on the island. Someone wearing a yellow rain slicker. They took off up the hill."

Nora rolled over and blinked a few times, then opened her eyes, squinting. She pushed herself to a seated position. "Say that again?"

Penny repeated the story. "I used the binoculars to get a better view. They had the hood up, though, so I couldn't see who it was."

"Do you think they arrived this morning?"

"Must have. They couldn't have been out here during the storm. There's no shelter besides these tents."

Nora raised an eyebrow. "You don't think someone was here without our knowledge, do you?"

"I'll go check the other tents," Penny offered. It was possible Lee had returned, or even Paige. Oliver had said she'd left Dublin, but Penny had assumed that Paige had been stuck on the mainland, unable to get out to Beag Anoach during the storm.

Penny ran to the other three tents, checking each one. The contents of Oliver's and Paige's tents appeared neat and undisturbed, the way they had left them. Lee's was also exactly the same. She wasn't surprised. If a member of the team had returned, surely they would have checked in with Penny and Nora.

When Penny went back to her tent, she found Nora up and dressed. "There's no sign that anyone has been here."

"That's what I figured." Nora put her shoes on. "Why don't we grab a quick breakfast and tour the island again? We'll check the boat landing first."

Penny hoped someone else was on the island so they could hitch a ride back to Anoach Island. *Someone of good will, that is. Not an antiquities thief.*

As she approached the dining area, Penny noticed that things seemed slightly off. Hadn't she left the kettle off the burner? It wasn't on, but she liked to be extra careful. And a plastic tub containing dry goods was sticking out from under the table. She usually tucked it underneath.

Penny pondered the situation for a moment, then shook herself. The weather last night had been so terrible and her actions so hasty that she might have left the kettle and tub that way.

She fed Corky, then made tea and foraged in the tub for a box of breakfast bars and oranges, which would make an easy meal with no dishes to clean afterward.

She and Nora ate quickly, then once again packed water bottles and snacks for their hike. They agreed that it was better to have food and drink and not need them than the reverse.

Corky appeared from a nearby clump of bushes, and Nora glanced at him, then swiveled in her seat to peer more closely. "What's wrong with his foot?"

At Nora's question, Penny noticed that the dog was limping, holding up his front paw.

"I have no idea," Penny said. "He was fine a few minutes ago."

"What's the matter, boy?" Nora crooned, going over to her dog. She sat on the ground and gently examined his paw. "Oh no. He cut his pad."

"Really?" Penny rushed over to examine the injury. "I'll get the first aid kit and some water and soap."

While Nora soothed her pet, Penny scurried to get the supplies.

Nora bathed the paw and wrapped it in bandages, then sighed. "He's going to have to stay here."

Penny's heart sank with disappointment for Corky, who loved going for walks. "I suppose so." She patted his head. "Your job today is to guard the place, Corky."

Nora rose to her feet. "We'd better tie him up. Otherwise, he'll try to follow us."

They left him in the shade of the dining canopy, his water dish and a bone to chew on in easy reach.

A few gentle whines followed the cousins as they walked away. Nora gritted her teeth. "It's for his own good. Right?"

"Definitely," Penny said. "We won't be gone that long, anyway." She hoped to be back before noon.

"Which way did the person you saw go?" Nora asked.

"Up the hill." Penny pointed. "Didn't you want to check the boat landing first?" That was in a different direction.

"That's right. I did." Nora veered toward the other path.

They went up and over the familiar rise, then started down the other side toward the dock. As soon as the landing came into view, they discovered that no one had secured a boat there. The dock was still empty.

"Okay, that's settled." Nora pivoted. "They must have tied up in the other cove. Or maybe someone dropped them off."

Penny spotted another trail leading through the grass and shrubs on top of the rise. "I bet that trail cuts over."

"It must," Nora said, adjusting her pack. "Let's find out."

They climbed the spine of the island, with visibility in all directions. They could see the entire bay, Anoach Island in one direction and the ocean beyond in the other. The weather had completely cleared, and the sky was deep blue, dotted with puffy clouds. The aroma of gorse rose from the warming soil, mingling with the salty breeze. Far below, waves resembled ruffles of lace as they ran to the shore.

"This is so beautiful." Penny stopped hiking and rotated slowly in place, taking in the full panorama. For a moment, she pushed all the mysteries, worries, and concerns out of her mind and enjoyed the experience.

Beside her, Nora was doing the same, using her phone to capture various vistas. Sometimes when she couldn't return to a place, she used photographs as inspiration for paintings.

"I'm refreshed," Nora said, tucking her phone away. "I needed that pause in the action."

When Finn arrived, Penny should bring him up to that point. Maybe they could have a picnic on the trail. As she and Nora ambled along, she thought about the itinerary they could enjoy during their time together. *This is more fun than thinking about murder.*

A little farther on, they reached a spot that overlooked the dig site. From there, Penny could clearly see the trenches, the tents, and the dining area—and a small, tan shape lying under the table, head on his paws.

"Aw, Corky," Nora said. "I hope he isn't too sad."

Penny handed her the binoculars. "Go ahead and check."

"Perfect." Nora took the glasses and focused on her pet. "He's napping."

"You know what's strange?" Penny mused. "Things were a little out of place in the dining area this morning. The kettle was on the burner and a tub was sticking out from under the table."

Nora, still gazing through the binoculars, said, "You never leave the kettle on the burner."

"It's not now, right?" Penny couldn't resist asking.

"Nope." Nora handed the binoculars back.

After some distance, the trail began to descend, taking them toward the cove they had explored before the storm. Penny's heart began to beat faster the closer they got. Would they find the slicker-clad person? Who was it—friend or foe?

They emerged onto an outcropping that gave them a view of the beach. A small motorboat was pulled up on the sand.

"Someone is here," Penny cried. "I wasn't imagining it."

"I never thought you were." Nora studied the boat. "Can I use those binoculars again?" Taking them from Penny and putting them to her eyes, she scanned the boat.

"What are you looking for?" Penny asked.

"Anything that might tell us who piloted that boat." Nora lowered the lenses and handed them back to Penny. "Nothing. It's empty."

"Too bad." Before putting the binoculars away, Penny scanned the cove. "No sign of anyone. I wonder where they are."

"Why don't we go find out?" Nora started picking her way down toward the shore.

The trail had become much steeper, so Penny had to concentrate on where she put her feet, especially in spots where the pebbles were loose. She had no desire to slide down the bumpy, rocky path to the bottom.

With a sigh of relief, she stepped onto the beach, appreciating the level footing, and followed Nora to the motorboat.

"Still no clues," Nora said once they examined the craft from bow to stern.

The boat was very similar to the one the dig team had used, Penny noticed. It could hold three or four people as well as some cargo.

"Maybe they'll give us a ride to Anoach Island," Penny suggested, eager to get off the smaller island.

Nora tilted her head and studied the rocky cliffs abutting the beach. "We can certainly ask." She threw Penny a smile. "For now, how do you feel about some more exploring?"

After studying the map, Nora went east along the beach and Penny went west. Their task was to see if they could find the cave mentioned in the Beag Anoach history. Nora had made Penny promise to not approach anyone until they were together. They were embarking on a strictly exploratory mission.

Penny skirted the cliff until she came to a spot where low-angled slabs touched the shore. Large boulders blocked a full view of the rock face, so she decided to climb up for a better vantage point. A cave opening might be behind one of the guardian rocks.

She left her pack on the beach, not wanting to be burdened by its weight in case the going got tricky. The steepness of the climb required her to lean over and use her hands in spots, her sneakers gripping the rock firmly enough that she wasn't afraid of falling. It was rather fun, actually.

Once she reached the boulders, she was able to explore along a wide ledge. Although she occasionally came upon a deep crevice, she didn't find any caves.

Penny climbed carefully back down to her pack. Perching on a rock, she drank some water, expecting Nora to be back any moment.

Five minutes went by, then ten. No Nora.

Penny was becoming concerned. She capped her bottle and put it away, then picked up the pack and walked down the beach, searching for the spot where Nora had started to climb.

Once she reached what she thought was the right area, she called for her cousin. "Nora? Where are you?"

The sole answer was the whistle of the wind and the waves gently breaking on the shore.

19

Penny waited a minute and then called again, thinking Nora should have been on her way back by that point. She found herself pacing down to the water and back, uncertain what to do. Was she overreacting? Perhaps the rocks blocked the sound of her voice. Every few seconds, she glanced up at the cliff, expecting to see her cousin returning, or at the very least to hear the scrape of sneakers on the rocks. Something. Anything.

Anxiety churning in her midsection, Penny set her pack down. She made sure that her phone was tucked safely in her jeans pocket and decided to keep the binoculars around her neck. They might come in handy.

She went up the rock face, soon finding a narrow path that Nora must have taken. In contrast to the ledges she'd traversed, it resembled an actual trail. Fortunately for her nerves, there weren't many spots where a sheer face fell away to the beach. She put out a hand to touch the rock wall and kept her eyes resolutely ahead, not daring to peek down.

A voice drifted toward her, the wind catching away the words. *Nora?* Was she talking to someone?

Penny edged closer, her steps slowing. *Fools rush in*, she reminded herself. In light of Caroline's death and Kenneth's hit-and-run, she had to be cautious.

The path led between two large boulders, narrowing to a point she could barely squeeze through. She was in the tightest spot when she heard voices again. Penny strained to listen and realized it was two women, but neither was Nora. She couldn't quite make out the words.

Penny wanted to rush the rest of the way through to find out who they were and if they had seen Nora. Again, innate caution urged her to remain concealed. How could she get a better view of them? If she continued through the crevice, they would probably see her. She couldn't take the risk.

A short distance back, she had noticed another route going in the same direction, although climbing somewhat higher. Perhaps that would allow her to get above the action.

Penny backed up with some difficulty and took the spur path, which was more of a clamber over rocks. The voices got louder as she proceeded, informing her she'd made the right decision.

The short path ended in a ledge overlooking a level area in front of a cave. Penny had to touch the wall to steady herself when she saw who was standing there.

Paige Matthews and Kinzi Eagan. There was an odd combination, but their body language told Penny they were well acquainted and comfortable together. Paige's words echoed in Penny's mind. *My grandmother's best friend.* Had she been referring to Kinzi? One or both of them must have been rustling around the campsite during the night, maybe searching for food.

A muffled cry caught Penny's ear, and both women faced the cave opening.

"I thought you gagged her," Kinzi said.

Paige took a step toward the opening. "I did."

Penny broke out in a cold sweat. *Her?* Were they talking about Nora? If only she could see into the cave.

Penny found that by crouching down and using the binoculars, she could peer inside. She gave a small gasp when she spotted Nora lying on the ground with hands and feet bound, a cloth around her mouth. While she watched in horror, Paige bent and tightened the gag.

"If you care about Penny at all," Paige scolded, "you'll stop trying to talk."

Because they would also tie Penny up and throw her into the cave if they crossed paths? What was Paige planning to do with Nora? Penny caught a glimpse of movement behind Nora. Moving the binoculars slightly, she identified the object as a man's sneaker. *Lee.* It had to be. Kinzi and Paige had taken Lee captive and had been keeping him here for the past couple of days. But why?

What were Paige and Kinzi up to?

Paige strode back out of the cave. "That should keep her quiet." She folded her arms and frowned at Kinzi. "You really got us into a pickle this time. You can't keep hitting people on the head."

Penny bit back a groan. Had Kinzi hurt Nora and Lee? How badly were they injured?

"They were going to find the Lady," Kinzi said, her voice a whine. "I couldn't allow that."

Paige tilted her head, regarding Kinzi. "I did something that could put me away for life because of you. I'm really beginning to regret it."

Penny's pulse leaped, and she held her breath.

"I didn't mean to push Caroline," Paige said. "All I was trying to do was watch out for you, the way I promised Grammie. She shouldn't have threatened to have you committed. She actually laughed when I confronted her. I lost my temper."

Penny could imagine the scene all too well. Caroline hadn't deserved to die, but her threat toward Kinzi was inhumane. Caroline wasn't related to Kinzi, nor had the woman done anything to her. So why had she gone that far?

"She was mad because I told her to leave the Lady alone," Kinzi said, pouting. "She had no right to try to take her from the museum."

"You did take the Lady," Paige pointed out.

Kinzi made a scoffing sound. "That's different. I'm protecting her. Caroline would have carried her away to London and dissected her."

"I don't think so." Paige sighed. "It's moot, anyway. Caroline is dead, and no one is taking the Lady anywhere."

Kinzi pointed into the cave, her finger trembling. "He was going to. He asked Barry the exact same questions Caroline did. He wanted to prove that the Lady is a fake. She's not. She's my ancestor. I told him and told him, and he wouldn't listen." The older woman was getting worked up now, her voice rising to a shriek.

"You didn't have to go this far," Paige said. "This is kidnapping, Kinzi."

"It's his own fault," Kinzi cried. "He sneaked up here and started poking around the cave. What else was I supposed to do? I couldn't let him find the Lady."

The missing bog body was in the cave. Penny hoped it had survived the journey intact, imagining Kinzi putting the remains in a boat and motoring over from Anoach Island under cover of night. Kinzi probably cleaned the museum, so she would have had access to the building after hours. The temptation to take the Lady must have proven to be too much.

"She belongs here." Kinzi was crying. "This was her home. Not some display case in a museum. Talk about undignified."

Penny could see her point. The remains being thousands of years old didn't negate the fact that they were human.

"You have to give the Lady back," Paige said in a soft voice, apparently unconvinced. "That's the first step in cleaning up this mess."

What were the other steps? Taking care of Nora and Lee somehow? Penny shuddered. She needed to get help, to get them out of the cave before they were hurt or killed. Penny patted her pocket, double-checking for her phone. She should go back down the trail and call for help.

As she edged back along the ledge, she heard Kinzi say, "I'm not giving her back. I'm going to cover the Lady with stones the way they did in the old days and put up a marker. I'll get an engraver to make something nice."

A lovely thought, Penny mused, although Kinzi would probably be in jail for theft, assault, and kidnapping soon. Caroline had probably regarded the woman as harmless if eccentric, more bluster than danger. What a miscalculation that had been on her part—and her miscalculations had included underestimating Paige.

Once she was sure they wouldn't notice her, Penny stood upright and hurried down the path, her heart pounding with urgency to call the Garda. Depending on how far away they were, it might take anywhere from minutes to an hour for them to arrive.

Penny was almost at the end of the spur trail when she saw another person climbing upward, head down and steps dogged. She recognized Barry Danvers quickly. Why was the museum director on Beag Anoach and headed toward the cave?

She must have made a sound because he raised his head and saw her.

"What are you doing here?" she asked.

A crafty expression slid across his face. "I could ask you the same." Resting one hand on his thigh, he took several deep inhales. "Trail is steep."

"How did you get here?" Penny asked, trying to subtly find out whether or not he was working with Kinzi and Paige. She pointed toward the cove. "Is that your boat?"

He shook his head. "Not mine. I tied up at the dock." He took out a handkerchief and dabbed his face. "It's quite a hike over."

That question answered, Penny continued moving. She had to call the Garda. "I wouldn't go up there if I were you," she warned. "People are getting hit on the head."

"What?" Barry gaped at her.

"Excuse me." She brushed past, staring at her phone to make sure she had a good signal. She also wanted to get out of reach, in case he tried to attack her.

"Wait, Penny," he called. "I need to talk to you."

She put up a finger to indicate she had something to do. Ducking around in the shelter of a good-sized boulder, she placed the call.

When dispatch answered, she gave her name and location. "We have a situation out here. Paige Matthews and Kinzi Eagan have taken my cousin and a man hostage. They're tied up in a cave above the south cove after being hit on the head. Their boat is there." Even to Penny's own ears, the story sounded far-fetched. "Please put me through to Detective Inspector Babcock. This is related to Caroline Pierce's murder."

"The inspector is not available. I can put you into her voice mail." The dispatcher remained calm and collected. She had probably heard it all.

"Please do. First, are you sending someone out here?"

"Yes, ma'am. We'll dispatch them right away. South side, you said?"

"That's right."

"Hold on, ma'am. I'll connect you to the inspector's voice mail."

After the tone, Penny hastily gave her name then said, "I overheard Paige Matthews confess to Caroline Pierce's murder." She gave Babcock the location and the information about Nora and Lee. After disconnecting, Penny texted the DI the same message.

When she emerged from around the boulder, Barry stood waiting for her. She must have looked alarmed because he put up his hands and said, "I come in peace." He cleared his throat. "I'm actually here to find the Lady."

"She's in the cave." Penny pointed up the hill. "I heard them talking about her."

Barry's brow furrowed. "Them?"

"Paige Matthews and Kinzi Eagan. I overheard Kinzi say that she stole the Lady."

He rubbed his chin. "I thought as much. Who else could it have been?"

Penny crossed her arms. "Maybe you."

He took a step back, his foot sliding on pebbles. Fortunately, he caught himself. "Why would I do that? Moving her might cause damage."

"Isn't it obvious?" Penny inquired. "You didn't want Caroline or Lee to investigate her provenance."

She expected denials and blustering. Instead, Barry hung his head. "You're right. I didn't. I would never destroy such a delicate and rare artifact, however."

"Your ancestor or his partner brought her here from Denmark, didn't they? They thought it was the perfect opportunity to put Beag Anoach on the map. People here have benefited ever since from the Lady's fame, even if she is a fraud."

Barry winced. "I know she is." He muttered something.

"What was that?" Penny asked.

He cleared his throat. "I found my ancestor's diary. He admitted to finding the Lady during a dig in Denmark. What a spectacular find. He'd spent years searching Ireland for something equally notable. The temptation was too much, I suppose. By claiming she was from here, he was able to fund a lot more work as well as promote Anoach Island."

So Barry had been sitting on the truth the entire time. If he had come clean, Caroline would still be alive. Penny decided it wasn't the right time to make him face the chain reaction he'd inadvertently caused. "Why didn't you tell anyone?" she asked instead. "That would have been the honest thing to do."

He ducked his head. "I had too much invested in the museum. And what about Muriel and her store? The bed-and-breakfast? Most of the businesses on Anoach use the Lady as a mascot for marketing."

"I get it, Barry." Penny wasn't totally unsympathetic to the man. No one would ever have known the truth, but then Caroline and Lee had come along and forced the issue.

Penny peered up the cliff. She really ought to go back up and monitor the situation. If Paige and Kinzi did anything else to Nora and Lee, she would tell them the Garda was on their way.

"You mentioned people getting hit," Barry said. "What did you mean?"

Penny had forgotten her warning. "My cousin and Lee are tied up in the cave. From what I overheard, I think Kinzi hit them both."

A funny expression crossed Barry's face. "Hit them?"

"Yes, on the head." Penny started up the path. "I'd better go see how they are doing." Her steps faltered. Why was Barry reacting so strangely? An insight burst into her mind. Purely on instinct, she asked, "Do you own a red car?"

His flushed face and shocked eyes told her the truth.

"You hit Kenneth," she said.

"It was an accident," he said, wringing his hands. "I didn't see him. He was dressed in brown. Plus, I was so distracted by Caroline's letter about the Lady. I panicked and drove away." He shook his head. "Not my finest moment."

"You have to tell the Garda," Penny urged. "It's better if you go to them."

"You're right. I know I should. Carroll Gleason figured it out, and he's been blackmailing me." Barry seemed almost relieved by the confession.

"I noticed he has a new boat," Penny said. "That's a crime too."

Between blackmail and unauthorized digging, the young man was in real trouble. She thought of another question. "Did you see me on camera when I was in the barn?"

Barry flushed. "I did. I had one up for that very reason, if someone discovered the car."

"Thought so." Penny gestured toward the other island. "I saw you driving the car on the headland."

"I was moving it to a new hiding place." Barry sighed. "Now that's finally over." After a moment, he pointed toward the cave. "What's going on up there? Can you fill me in?"

Penny quickly gave him the gist of what she had overheard. "I'm worried about what they might do to Nora and Lee. I mean, Paige pushed Caroline off the cliff." Her heart thumped. What if she did the same to Nora? "I'd better go."

"I'll help," Barry said. "Between the two of us, we'll get it sorted."

Was he offering to help? If so, Penny accepted. "What do you have in mind?"

They conferred for a couple of minutes, batting ideas around. Since the Garda was en route, Penny's main concern was reaching Nora and Lee and keeping them safe. The Garda could catch up with Paige and Kinzi.

Before heading up the cliff to the cave, they detoured down to the beach at Barry's suggestion. He went over to the outboard motor and tinkered with it while Penny waited.

When he returned, she asked, "What did you do?"

He held out his hand, grimy from his work with the engine. Sitting in his palm was a spark plug. "That boat won't be going anywhere."

"Good work, Barry." Eager to get going, Penny started up the trail, Barry right behind her. She had the feeling that helping her was a way for him to redeem himself somewhat.

Once they reached the point where the spur trail jutted off, they halted. Penny would climb to the lookout point while Barry approached the cave. "Are you ready?" she asked Barry.

Barry tugged at his shirt collar. "Ready as I'll ever be. Wish me luck."

20

Penny practically ran up the spur trail. When she approached the overlook, she stopped so she wouldn't be observed. She took her binoculars out and trained them on the cave.

Her shoulders sagged in relief. Nora and Lee were still there, and she could see both of them moving.

Paige and Kinzi sat outside the cave, eating baked beans from cans. "We need to get out of here," Paige said.

"Not unless we bring the Lady," Kinzi said, a stubborn tone in her voice. "I'm not going anywhere without her."

Paige stirred her beans, an annoyed expression on her face. "We can't take her. She requires special handling. We should leave her here and come back later." She made a face. "I really don't like beans."

Kinzi gestured with her thumb. "What about them? Are we leaving them behind too?"

The younger woman shook her head. "They have to go. Unless you'd like to spend the rest of your life in jail."

"No way," Kinzi squawked. "I don't have that much time left." She gave a hoarse chuckle. "What a turn of events that would be. I free the Lady and end up in a cage myself."

Mentally, Penny urged Barry to move faster. They had barely come back in the nick of time to save Nora and Lee.

Penny heard huffing and puffing as Barry entered the clearing. "Good afternoon, ladies," he said.

Paige jumped, and the can of beans went flying, the contents spilling out. She put a hand to her chest. "You scared me."

"Sorry about that." Barry wiped his forehead with his handkerchief. "Warm day, isn't it?"

Kinzi, meanwhile, had leaped up and was guarding the cave opening with her arms and legs spread wide. "You can't have her."

"Okay," Barry said, drawing out the word as if he had no idea what she was talking about. "I was out taking a little stroll and ended up here. The doctor told me I should get more exercise." He scanned the area as if taking everything in, careful not to look directly at the cave. "Busy day on Beag Anoach. The Garda were arriving as I reached the height of land. Wonder what they're up to."

Paige's eyes narrowed into slits. "Did you say the Garda?"

"Uh-huh." Barry pursed his lips. "They had quite a team. Even a dog. Must be searching for someone. Heard that Lee fellow from the dig is missing, so maybe they're trying to find him."

Penny had to hand it to Barry. That was a nice touch, as was the mention of a tracking dog.

Kinzi and Paige exchanged glances. Moving with almost comically slow steps, Kinzi picked up a backpack. "I've had enough sunshine and fresh air for today. Want to head back to the mainland, Paige?"

"Sure thing." Paige picked up a yellow slicker and her own bag.

"See you later, Barry," Kinzi said. "Enjoy your day."

"I will," he said with a big grin as he took a seat on a rock. "Have a good trip."

The two women walked at a normal pace out of the clearing. Then Penny heard the pounding of footsteps as they broke into a run.

Smiling, she waited until she judged they were well down the trail, then she hurried to join Barry.

"Good job," she called as she burst into the clearing. Then she stopped short. "Where are you, Barry?"

"In here," he called from the cave.

Penny ran to the cave opening, dropping her pack outside. "Nora, are you okay?"

"I'm fine," Nora said. She was sitting up and drinking from her own water bottle. Her hands were free, but her feet were still tied with nylon cord.

Barry was unbinding Lee's hands using a pocketknife to cut the cord. "He's in bad shape," he said tersely. "Barely conscious. Quite the wound on his head."

"Oh no." Penny moved closer so she could see the young man. He lay with his eyes closed on the stone floor. Barry had removed his gag.

"I'm alive," Lee whispered, his eyes still shut. "I have a huge headache. And I'm starving."

"Better leave him lying flat until the medics come," Nora said. "They are coming, right?"

"I assume so," Penny said. "I told them you two were kidnapped."

"Sorry, mate," Barry told Lee. "We have to hold off on food and water a little while longer." He cut the cord around Lee's ankles, then Nora's.

"Thanks, Barry." Nora stretched her legs as she capped her water. "I saw you up on the ledge, Penny. I knew then that everything would be all right."

Penny sat down beside her cousin and hugged her, tears of relief flooding her eyes. Nora leaned in and Penny saw a few tears in her eyes as well.

"Too bad they got away," Nora said. "I understand the strategy, though. You saved us."

Penny and Barry laughed. "Not quite," Barry said. "There's the matter of a missing spark plug." He showed it to Nora. "This is from their boat's engine. They're not going anywhere."

Penny glanced toward the cave opening. "Is there a way to see the cove from here?"

"A trail to the right of the cave leads to an overlook," Barry said.

"Be right back." Penny scrambled out of the cave. She readily found the path. After a short climb, she was perched above the beach in a sheltered overhang. She briefly wondered if smugglers had watched for ships to come in from the same point, and decided they probably had.

Lifting her binoculars, Penny scanned the shore and spotted Paige and Kinzi. They had pushed the boat into the water and were drifting, trying to get the motor to start. It was readily apparent they were arguing. Paige picked up an oar and started to paddle.

A boat engine rumbled a moment before a Garda craft roared into view, effectively cutting off their escape. Even from that distance, Penny could see their shocked faces as they realized that Barry hadn't told them the truth about the Garda's whereabouts.

While Penny watched, a garda at the bow of the police boat called out through a megaphone, "Put your hands up. You are under arrest."

The two women raised their hands slowly. Kinzi lurched as if to dive overboard, but Paige reached out and tugged her back into her seat.

An inflatable raft was lowered into the water, and several officers climbed aboard. Penny noticed a familiar figure still on board the larger ship, and her heart skipped a beat. It was Finn, dressed in civilian clothes.

She jumped to her feet and began waving her arms, hoping he would notice her. After a few moments, a uniformed garda elbowed him and pointed.

It didn't take the binoculars to see the grin stretch across his face. He waved back, then conferred with the other garda. Penny guessed he was asking to come ashore.

When he did step onto the beach, Penny planned to be there to greet him. She rushed back along the path. "The Garda are here," she cried as she reached the cave. "And guess what, Nora? Finn is with them."

"Marvelous," Nora said. "Want to go down to meet them?"

"I do." Penny paused. "But I should stay with you. He'll understand."

Nora levered herself to her feet. "I'm coming too. I need to move around."

"Barry, are you all right waiting here?" Penny asked.

The older man sat beside Lee, keeping an eye on him. He waved off her concern. "Absolutely. You need to guide them to the cave."

Penny and Nora headed down the trail, Nora moving slowly at first. After a couple of minutes, her muscles loosened up and she became more limber.

"Is your head okay?" Penny asked.

Nora rubbed the back of her head. "It's fine. It's a small bump. It was more surprising than anything. Plus, there were two of them."

Penny shuddered. "How awful. I'm so sorry you went through that."

"Me too," Nora said ruefully. "However, we have now solved two crimes in one go. How's that for a record?"

"Three," Penny crowed. "Barry confessed to hitting Kenneth with his car. He said it was an accident and he panicked. He's going to come clean."

"His help today might mitigate his sentence," Nora said. "He really came through when it mattered."

Penny agreed. "It was a brilliant plan. Better than having to fight hand to hand to subdue Paige and Kinzi. I would have, though. For you."

"As would I." Nora made fighting movements with her fists, and they both laughed.

While they had been hiking down, Penny had heard the inflatable boat motoring back and forth to the main ship. Hopefully Finn would already be on the beach. They were almost down when she paused and ran her fingers through her hair, wishing she had a mirror and conscious that she really needed a shower and a shampoo.

"Don't fuss, Penny." Nora's face crinkled with humor. "You have the perfect lost-in-the-wilderness appearance."

"Oh, you." Penny swiped at her cousin, then at the dust marring the knees and seat of her jeans. That was the best she could do, unfortunately.

Finally, they stepped down onto the sand. Penny took in the scene. Kinzi and Paige were on shore, handcuffed. Gardaí swarmed around, a group that included two medics heading toward Penny and Nora. Finn stood beside Detective Inspector Babcock, who was directing the action. And, at the far end of the cove, a dog appeared, running with periodic hitches to his injured paw. The bandage was dangling, dirty and half off, and his leash trailed from his collar. He'd escaped from the campsite to find them.

"Corky!" Nora cried.

The dog's tail whipped back and forth as he hobbled toward his owner and she ran to meet him. Pet and owner greeted each other with great joy, though Nora peppered her terms of endearment with a scolding for running on an injured paw. He responded by licking her face.

Finn glanced toward Penny, and their eyes met. He said a quick word to Babcock and strode across the sand. "There you are," he said. "I've been looking for you."

"And I've been waiting for you."

He swept her into his arms and gave her a thorough kiss. Then he pulled back, hands on her shoulders. "I can't wait to hear what you've been up to."

"I hope you have a few hours," she said cheekily. "We solved all three crimes, Finn."

Shaking his head, he gave her another quick hug. "You are amazing, not that I'm surprised anymore." He slung his arm around her shoulders. "Let's go give Detective Inspector Babcock the update."

The next day, Penny and Finn happily paddled kayaks around Beag Anoach, enjoying the sunshine and fresh sea air. They planned to pull ashore for a picnic and a ramble around the dig site.

They'd finally left Beag Anoach late the previous day, remaining on-site until the Garda rescued Lee and wrapped up the crime scene at the cave. The Lady had been retrieved, under the care of Oliver and other experts who rushed in. She was back at the museum in controlled conditions, with everyone waiting to learn her fate.

As promised, Barry confessed to the hit-and-run. He would face consequences, although his assistance with Kinzi and Paige would hopefully lessen them.

Paige admitted to the Garda that she had killed Caroline. She said they had been arguing about Kinzi, with Paige urging Caroline to leave the woman alone. Caroline had replied that she was planning to report Kinzi to the Garda for threats, with the possible outcome that she would be examined for mental fitness. That was when they struggled—and Caroline ended up falling off the cliff. Without witnesses, it would probably be ruled manslaughter. Paige also identified the key chain found on the cliff as hers.

Penny and Finn passed by the south cove. The little beach was deserted, the crescent of sand inviting. It was hard to believe that mere hours before, teams of Garda had stormed the shore and arrested three people.

Lee had been taken to the hospital, where he was treated and released to rest at the caravan park. He wouldn't be returning to the dig.

Oliver had fired him for prioritizing a personal side project over his work on the dig. Lee took it in stride and planned to focus on writing a book about the Lady. He'd rallied enough to request access to Barry's ancestor's diary, promising a share of income related to the project. Barry would probably need it for his legal defense.

Penny and Finn paddled side by side around the east side of the island, their destination the cove with the dock. A boat was tied there, the one that had been missing and found adrift between the islands. Carroll had set it free to make life more difficult for Penny and Nora. Found hiding out in his friend's cottage, Carroll had been arrested on charges of blackmail and trespassing, and his friend who had raided the dig site with him had already confessed to the attempted break-in at Kenneth's caravan.

Fortunately, the boat had been found drifting instead of smashed up on the rocks as it could have been during the storm.

At the cove, they navigated the slender kayaks right to the shore, where Finn pulled them up securely on the sand. Penny climbed out, her water shoes splashing in the water. She retrieved her dry bag from inside so she could change into sneakers. They left their life jackets, gloves, helmets, and paddles with the boats.

"I want to see the spot where you found the gold," Finn said, his eyes glowing with interest. "That must have been the thrill of a lifetime."

"It certainly was." A positive thrill, instead of a frightening one. Penny smiled. *Just like being with Finn.* They were so comfortable in each other's company, yet every time their eyes met, Penny's heart leaped.

Penny carried the bag containing their sandwiches while Finn carted the beverages. They hiked to the rise, where they stopped to view the dig below. Oliver and Nora were working together, the last members left of the team. Corky lay nearby, supervising.

They went down the hill, stopping at the dining area to drop off lunch for Oliver and Nora. Then Penny gave Finn a tour of the dig, pointing out various features of the former settlement.

"How was the kayaking?" Oliver asked when they reached the trench where he dug while Nora sifted.

"Spectacular," Penny said. "We went all the way around the island." She rotated her shoulders. "I'm glad it's not any larger."

"Good exercise, for sure." Oliver pushed his trowel into the earth. "Ready for a break, Nora?"

Nora wiped her arm across her forehead. "Definitely. It's getting hot out here."

"Show them what we found," Oliver said, throwing a grin at Nora.

Nora bent down and picked up a box, then held it out. Inside was a slender gold bracelet. "We think this is related to the hoard. Oliver never expected to find it here."

Penny gasped at the object's beauty. "Does this mean another trip to Dublin?"

"I'm afraid so," Oliver said. "Where I also plan to hold interviews for the team in Kenneth's stead. It's down to me and Kenneth until the university sends replacements, and even four isn't enough."

"How is Kenneth?" Penny asked.

"He's getting out of the hospital in a couple of days," Oliver said. "He won't be mobile enough to dig for a while, but he'll handle all the paperwork. I'm hoping he'll feel up to the Dublin trips. I really want to be digging and finding more such treasures."

"I'll send you those contacts for private security I mentioned at dinner last night," Finn said. "Sounds like you might need it if you keep unearthing finds like this."

"I'll certainly need help since I won't have Penny and Nora around," Oliver joked. Corky whined. "Or you, Corky."

"There's a bit of other news," Nora said. "My illustrations are going to be included in a publication about the dig that Oliver is writing."

"That's wonderful." Penny beamed. Despite murder, a hit-and-run, and much mayhem, joining the dig had been personally—and in Nora's case, professionally—rewarding. "I brought enough lunch for four. Would you like to join us?"

"I'd love to," Oliver said. "Thank you."

As they set off toward the dining area, Penny took Finn's hand. Glancing up at the headland, she imagined a lady standing there—the real one who had worn the bracelet.

What would she think of their efforts to uncover and preserve a long-distant past? Penny thought that she would probably approve. No one wanted to be forgotten.

YOUR FEEDBACK MEANS A LOT TO US!

Up to this point, we've been doing all the writing. Now it's *your* turn!

Tell us what you think about this book, the characters, the plot, or anything else you'd like to share with us about this series. We can't wait to hear from *you*!

Log on to give us your feedback at:
https://www.surveymonkey.com/r/IrishTearoom

Annie's FICTION